A Russian Affair

ANTON CHEKHOV

A Russian Affair

GREAT 🐧🐧 LOVES

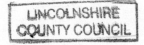
PENGUIN BOOKS

Published by the Penguin Group
Penguin Books Ltd, 80 Strand, London WC2R ORL, England
Penguin Group (USA) Inc., 375 Hudson Street, New York, New York 10014, USA
Penguin Group (Canada), 90 Eglinton Avenue East, Suite 700, Toronto, Ontario, Canada M4P 2Y3
(a division of Pearson Penguin Canada Inc.)
Penguin Ireland, 25 St Stephen's Green, Dublin 2, Ireland
(a division of Penguin Books Ltd)
Penguin Group (Australia), 250 Camberwell Road, Camberwell, Victoria 3124, Australia
(a division of Pearson Australia Group Pty Ltd)
Penguin Books India Pvt Ltd, 11 Community Centre, Panchsheel Park, New Delhi – 110 017, India
Penguin Group (NZ), 67 Apollo Drive, Rosedale, North Shore 0632, New Zealand
(a division of Pearson New Zealand Ltd)
Penguin Books (South Africa) (Pty) Ltd, 24 Sturdee Avenue,
Rosebank, Johannesburg 2196, South Africa

Penguin Books Ltd, Registered Offices: 80 Strand, London WC2R ORL, England

www.penguin.com

First published in *The Lady with the Little Dog and Other Stories, 1896–1904*, 2002
This selection published in Penguin Books 2007

1

Translation copyright © Ronald Wilks 1982, 1986, 2002

Typeset by Rowland Phototypesetting Ltd, Bury St Edmunds, Suffolk
Printed in England by Clays Ltd, St Ives plc

978-0-141-03285-6

Contents

Anton Pavlovich Chekhov (1860–1904) was born in Taganrog, a port on the Sea of Azov. He received a classical education at the Taganrog Gymnasium, then in 1879 he went to Moscow, where he entered the medical faculty of the university, graduating in 1884. His most famous stories were written after his return from the convict island of Sakhalin, which he visited in 1890. For five years he lived on his small country estate near Moscow, but when his health began to fail he moved to the Crimea. After 1900, the rest of his life was spent at Yalta, where he met Tolstoy and Gorky. He wrote very few stories during the last years of his life, devoting most of his time to a thorough revision of the stories, of which the first comprehensive edition was published in 1899–1901, and to the writing of his great plays. In 1901 Chekhov married Olga Knipper, an actress of the Moscow Art Theatre. He died of consumption in 1904.

About Love

They had delicious pies, crayfish and mutton chops for lunch, and during the meal Nikanor, the cook, came upstairs to inquire what the guests would like for dinner. He was a man of medium height, puffy-faced and with small eyes. He was so close-shaven his whiskers seemed to have been plucked out and not cut off with a razor.

Alyokhin told his guests that the beautiful Pelageya was in love with the cook. However, since he was a drunkard and a brawler, she didn't want to marry him; but she did not object to 'living' with him, as they say. He was a very devout Christian, however, and his religious convictions would not allow him to 'set up house' with her. So he insisted on marriage and would not hear of anything else. He cursed her when he was drunk and even beat her. When he was like this, she would hide upstairs and sob, and then Alyokhin and his servants would not leave the house in case she needed protecting. They began to talk about love.

Alyokhin started: 'What makes people fall in love and why couldn't Pelageya fall for someone else, someone more suited to her mentally and physically, instead of that ugly-mug Nikanor (everyone round here calls him ugly-mug), since *personal* happiness is so important in love? It's a mystery, and you can interpret it which way you like. Only one indisputable truth has been said about love up to now, that it's a "tremendous mystery", and everything else that's been written or said about it has never provided an answer and is just a reformulation of problems that have always remained unsolved. One theory that might, on the face of it, explain one case, won't explain a dozen others. Therefore, in my opinion, the best way is to treat each case individually, without making generalizations. In doctors' jargon, you have to "isolate" each case.'

'Absolutely true,' Burkin said.

'Decent Russians like ourselves have a passion for problems that have never been solved. Usually, love is poeticized, beautified with roses and nightingales, but we Russians have to flavour it with the "eternal problems" – and we choose the most boring ones at that.

'When I was still studying in Moscow I had a "friend", a dear lady who'd be wondering how much I'd allow her every month and how much a pound of beef was while I held her close. And *we* never stop asking ourselves questions when we love: is it honourable or dishonourable, clever or stupid, how will it all end, and so on. Whether that's a good thing or not, I don't know, but I do know that it cramps your style, doesn't provide any satisfaction and gets on your nerves.'

It looked as if he wanted to tell us a story. It's always the same with people living on their own – they have something that they are only too pleased to get off their chests. Bachelors living in town go to the public baths and restaurants just to talk to someone, and sometimes they tell the bath attendants or waiters some very interesting stories. Out in the country they normally pour out their hearts to their guests. Through the windows we could only see grey skies now and trees dripping with rain – in this kind of weather there was really nowhere to go and nothing else to do except listen to stories.

'I've been living and farming in Sofino for quite a long time now – since I left university, in fact,' Alyokhin began. 'I was never brought up to do physical work and I'm an "armchair" type by inclination. When I first came to this estate they were up to their eyes in debts. But since my father had run up these debts partly through spending so much on my education, I decided to stay and work on the estate until the debts were paid off. That was my decision and I started working here – not without a certain degree of aversion, I must confess. The soil's not very fertile round here, and to avoid farming at a loss you have to rely on serfs or hire farm labourers, which more or less comes to the same thing. Or else you have to run your own estate peasant-style, which means you yourself and all your family have to slave away in the fields. There's no two ways about it. But then I didn't have time for subtleties: I didn't leave a square inch of soil unturned, I rounded up all the peasants and their wives from neighbouring villages and we all worked like mad. I did the ploughing, sowing and reaping myself, which was a terrible bore and it made me screw my face up in disgust, like the starving village cat forced to eat cucumbers in some kitchen garden. I was all aches and pains and I'd fall asleep standing up. From the very beginning I thought that I'd have no trouble at all combining this life of slavery with my cultural activities. All I had to do, so I thought, was keep to some settled routine. So I installed myself in the best rooms up here, had coffee and liqueurs after lunch and dinner, and took the *European Herald* with me to bed. But our parish priest, Father Ivan, turned up and polished off all my liqueurs at one sitting. And the *European Herald* ended up with his daughters, since during the summer, especially when we were harvesting, I never made it to my own bed but had to sleep in a barn, on a sledge, or in a woodman's hut somewhere, so what time was there for reading? Gradually I moved downstairs, had meals with the servants – they were all that was left of my earlier life of luxury – the same servants who had waited on my father and whom I did not have the heart to dismiss.

'In my early years here I was made honorary justice of the peace. This meant occasional trips into town, taking my seat at the sessions and local assizes, and this made a break for me. When you're stuck in a place like this for two or three months at a stretch – especially in the winter – you end up pining for your black frock-coat. I saw frock-coats – and uniforms and tailcoats as well – at the assizes. They were all lawyers, educated men there, people I could talk to. After sleeping on a sledge or eating with the servants it was the height of luxury sitting in an armchair, with clean underwear, light boots, and a watch-chain on your chest!

'They gave me a warm welcome in town and I eagerly made friends. The most significant, and frankly, the most pleasant, of these friendships was with Luganovich, vice-president of the assizes. Both of you know him, he's a most delightful man. Now, all this was about the time of that famous arson case. The questioning went on for two days and we were exhausted. Luganovich took a look at me and said, "Do you know what? Come and have dinner at my place."

'This was right out of the blue, as I didn't know him at all well, only through official business, and I'd never been to his house. I went to my hotel room for a quick change and went off to dinner. Now I had the chance to meet Luganovich's wife, Anna Alekseyevna. She was still very young then, not more than twenty-two, and her first child had been born six months before. It's all finished now and it's hard for me to say exactly what it was I found so unusual about her, what attracted me so much, but at the time, over dinner, it was all so clear, without a shadow of doubt: here was a young, beautiful, kind, intelligent, enchanting woman, unlike any I'd met before. Immediately I sensed that she was a kindred spirit, someone I knew already, and that her face, with its warm clever eyes, was just like one I had seen before when I was a little boy, in an album lying on my mother's chest of drawers.

'At the trial four Jews had been convicted of arson and conspiracy – in my opinion, on no reasonable grounds at all. I became very heated over dinner, felt bad and I can't remember even now what I said, only that Anna Alekseyevna kept shaking her head and telling her husband, "Dmitry, how *can* they do this?"

'Luganovich was a good man, one of those simple,

open-hearted people who are firmly convinced that once you have a man in the dock he *must* be guilty, and that a verdict can only be challenged in writing, according to the correct legal procedure, and *never* during dinner or private conversation. "*We* haven't set anything alight," he said softly, "so *we* won't have to stand trial or go to prison."

'Both husband and wife plied me with food and drink. Judging from little details – the way they made coffee together and their mutual understanding that needed no words – I concluded that they were living peacefully and happily, and that they were glad to have a guest. After dinner there were piano duets. When it grew dark I went back to the hotel. All of this was at the beginning of spring. I spent the whole of the following summer in Sofino without emerging once and I was too busy even to think of going into town. But I could not forget that slender, fair-haired woman for one moment. Although I made no conscious effort to think about her, she seemed to cast a faint shadow over me.

'In late autumn there was a charity show in town. I took my seat in the governor's box, where I'd been invited during the interval, and there was Anna Alekseyevna sitting next to the governor's wife. Once again I was struck by that irresistible, radiant beauty, by those tender, loving eyes, and once again I felt very close to her.

'We sat side by side, then we went into the foyer where she told me, "You've lost weight. Have you been ill?"

'"Yes, I've rheumatism in my shoulder and I sleep badly when it rains."

'"You look quite exhausted. When you came to dinner in the spring you seemed younger, more cheerful. You were very lively then and said some most interesting things. I was even a little taken with you, I must confess. For some reason I often thought about you during the summer and when I was getting ready for the theatre I had a feeling I might see you today." And she burst out laughing.

'"But now you seem to have no energy," she repeated. "It ages you."

'Next day I had lunch with the Luganoviches. Afterwards they drove out to their country villa to make arrangements for the winter, and I went with them. I came back to town with them and at midnight I was having tea in those peaceful domestic surroundings, in front of a roaring fire, while the young mother kept slipping out to see if her little girl was sleeping. Afterwards I made a point of visiting the Luganoviches whenever I came to town. We grew used to one another and I usually dropped in unannounced, like one of the family.

'That soft drawling voice I found so attractive would come echoing from one of the far rooms: "Who's there?"

'"It's Pavel Konstantinych," the maid or nanny would reply.

'Then Anna Alekseyevna would appear with a worried look and every time she'd ask me the same question, "Why haven't you been to see us? Is anything wrong?"

7

'The way she looked at me, the delicate, noble hand she offered me, the clothes she wore in the house, her hairstyle, her voice and footsteps always made me feel that something new, out of the ordinary and important had happened in my life. We'd have long conversations – and long silences – immersed in our own thoughts. Or she would play the piano for me. If she was out, I'd stay and wait, talk to the nanny, play with the baby, or lie on the sofa in the study and read the papers. When Anna Alekseyevna came back I'd meet her in the hall, take her shopping and for some reason I'd always carry it so devotedly and exultantly you'd have thought I was a little boy.

'You know the story about the farmer's wife who had no worries until she went and bought a pig. The Luganoviches had no worries, so they made friends with me. If I was away from town for long, they thought I must be ill or that something had happened to me and they would get terribly worked up. And they were concerned that an educated man like myself, speaking several languages, didn't use his time studying or doing literary work and could live out in the wilds, forever turning round like a squirrel on a wheel and slaving away without a penny to show for it. They sensed that I was deeply unhappy and that if I spoke, laughed or ate, it was only to hide my suffering. Even at cheerful times, when I was in good spirits, I knew they were giving me searching looks. They were particularly touching when I really was in trouble, when some creditor was chasing me, or when I couldn't pay some bill on time. Both of them would stay by the window whispering, and then the husband would come over to me, looking serious, and say, "Pavel Konstantinych, if you're a bit short, my wife and I *beg* you not to think twice about asking us!"

'And his ears would turn red with excitement. Often, after a whispering session at the window, he would come over to me, ears flushed, and say, "My wife and I *beg* you to accept this little gift."

'And he'd give me cufflinks, a cigarette case or a table-lamp. In return, I'd send them some poultry, butter or flowers from the country. They were quite well-off, by the way, both of them. In my younger days I was always borrowing and wasn't too fussy where the money came from, taking it wherever I could get it. But for nothing in the world would I have borrowed from the Luganoviches. The very idea!

'I was unhappy. Whether I was at home, out in the fields, in the barn, I couldn't stop thinking about *her*, and I tried to unravel the mystery of that young, beautiful, clever woman who had married an uninteresting man, who could almost be called old (he was over forty) and had borne his children. And I tried to solve the enigma of that boring, good-natured, simple-minded fellow, with his insufferable common sense, always crawling up to the local stuffed shirts at balls and soirées, a lifeless, useless man whose submissive, indifferent expression made you think he'd been brought along as an object for sale, a man who believed, however, that he had the right to be happy and to be the father of *her* children. I never gave up trying to understand why she was fated to meet him, and not me, why such a horrible mistake should have to occur in *our* lives.

'Every time I went into town I could tell from her eyes that she had been waiting for me, and she would admit that from the moment she'd got up she'd had some kind of premonition that I would be coming. We had long talks and there were long silences, and we didn't declare our love, but concealed it jealously, timidly, fearing anything that might betray our secret to each other. Although I loved her tenderly, deeply, I reasoned with myself and tried to guess what the consequences would be if we had no strength to combat it. It seemed incredible that my gentle, cheerless love could suddenly rudely disrupt the happy lives of her husband and children – of that whole household in fact, where I was so loved and trusted. Was I acting honourably? She would have gone away with me, but where could I take her? It would have been another matter if my life had been wonderful and eventful – if, for example, I'd been fighting to liberate my country, or if I'd been a famous scholar, actor or artist. But I'd only be taking her away from an ordinary, pedestrian life into one that was just the same, just as prosaic, even more so, perhaps. And just how long would we stay happy? What would become of her if I was taken ill, or died? Or if we simply stopped loving each other?

'And she seemed to have come to the same conclusion. She had been thinking about her husband, her children, and her mother, who loved her husband like a son. If she were to let her feelings get the better of her, then she would have to lie or tell the whole truth, but either alternative would have been equally terrible and distressing for someone in her position. And she was tormented by the question: would her love make me happy, wouldn't she be complicating a life which was difficult enough already, brimful of all kinds of unhappiness? She thought that she was no longer young enough for me and that she wasn't hard-working or energetic enough to start a new life with me. Often she told her husband that I should marry some nice clever girl who would make a good housewife and be a help to me. But immediately she would add that it would be a hard job finding someone answering to that description in *that* town.

'Meanwhile the years passed. Anna Alekseyevna already had two children. Whenever I called on the Luganoviches the servants welcomed me with smiles, the children shouted that Uncle Pavel Konstantinych had arrived and clung to my neck. Everyone was glad. They didn't understand what was going on deep down inside me and they thought that I too shared their joy. All of them considered me a most noble person, and both parents and children felt that the very personification of nobility was walking around the house, and this lent a very special charm to their attitude towards me, as if my being there made their lives purer and finer. I would go to the theatre with Anna Alekseyevna – we always used to walk. We would sit side by side in the stalls, shoulders touching, and as I took the opera glasses from her I felt that she was near and dear to me, that she belonged to me, that we couldn't live without each other. But through some strange lack of mutual understanding we would always say goodbye and part like strangers when we left the theatre. In that town they were already saying God knows what about us, but there wasn't one word of truth in it.

'Later on, Anna Alekseyevna visited her mother and sister more often. She started to have fits of depression when she realized her life was unfulfilled, ruined, and she had no desire to see either her husband or the children. She was already having treatment for a nervous disorder.

'We didn't say one word to each other and she seemed strangely irritated with me when other people were around. She'd quarrel with everything I said, and if I was having an argument she would always take the other person's side. If I dropped something she would coldly say, "Congratulations." If I left my opera glasses behind when we went to the theatre she'd say afterwards, "I *knew* that you'd forget them."

'Whether for better or for worse, there's nothing in this life that doesn't come to an end sooner or later. The time to part finally came when Luganovich was made a judge in one of the western provinces. They had to sell the furniture, horses and the villa. When we drove out to the villa and turned round for a last glimpse of the garden and the green roof, everyone felt sad and it was then I realized the time had come to say farewell – and not only to a simple villa. On the advice of her doctor they decided to send Anna Alekseyevna to the Crimea, while soon afterwards Luganovich would take the children with him to the western province.

'A large crowd of us went to see Anna Alekseyevna off. She had already said goodbye to her husband and children, and the train was about to leave at any moment. I rushed to her compartment to put a basket that she'd almost forgotten onto the luggage-rack. Now it was time to say farewell. When our eyes met we could hold ourselves back no longer. I embraced her and she pressed her face to my chest and the tears just flowed. As I kissed her face, shoulders and hands that were wet with tears – oh, how miserable we both were! – I declared my love and realized, with a searing pain in my heart, how unnecessary, trivial and illusory everything that had stood in the way of our love had been. I understood that with love, if you start theorizing about it, you must have a nobler, more meaningful starting-point than mere happiness or unhappiness, sin or virtue, as they are commonly understood. Otherwise it's best not to theorize at all.

'I kissed her for the last time, pressed her hand and we parted for ever. The train was already moving. I took a seat in the next compartment, which was empty, and cried until the first stop, where I got out and walked back to Sofino.'

While Alyokhin was telling his story the rain had stopped and the sun had come out. Burkin and Ivan Ivanych went onto the balcony, from which there was a wonderful view of the garden and the river, gleaming like a mirror now in the sunlight. As they admired the view they felt sorry that this man, with those kind, clever eyes, who had just told his story so frankly, was really turning round and round in his huge estate like

into the grounds of a manor house that was unfamiliar to me. The sun was already sinking and the evening shadows lay across the flowering rye. Two rows of closely planted, towering fir trees stood like solid, unbroken walls, forming a handsome, sombre avenue. I easily climbed the fence and walked down the avenue, slipping on pine needles that lay about two inches deep on the ground. It was quiet and dark – only high up in the tree tops a vivid golden light quivered here and there and transformed spiders' webs into shimmering rainbows. The smell of resin from the firs was almost stifling. Then I turned into a long avenue of lime trees. And here too all was neglect and age. Last year's leaves rustled sadly underfoot and in the dusk shadows lurked between the trees. In the old fruit orchard to the right an oriole sang feebly, reluctantly, most probably because he too was old. But then the limes ended. I went past a white house with a terrace and a kind of mezzanine or attic storey – and suddenly a vista opened up: a courtyard, a large pond with bathing place, a clump of green willows, and a village on the far bank, with a slender, tall bell-tower whose cross glittered in the setting sun. For one fleeting moment I felt the enchantment of something very close and familiar to me, as though I had once seen this landscape as a child.

At the white stone gates that led from the courtyard into open country – sturdy, old-fashioned gates surmounted by lions – two young girls were standing. One of them – the elder, who was slim, pale and very pretty, with a mass of auburn hair and a small stubborn mouth – wore a stern expression and hardly looked at me. But the other girl, still very young – no more than seventeen or eighteen – similarly slim and pale, with large mouth and big eyes, looked at me in astonishment as I passed by. She said something in English and seemed embarrassed. And it seemed that I had long known these two charming faces. I returned home with the feeling that it had all been a lovely dream.

Soon afterwards when I was strolling with Belokurov one day around noon by the house, a light sprung carriage suddenly drove into the yard, rustling over the grass: in it was one of the girls – the elder. She was collecting money for some villagers whose houses had burnt down. Without looking at us she gave a serious, detailed report about how many houses had burnt down in the village of Siyanov, how many women and children had been left homeless and what immediate measures the relief committee (to which she now belonged) was proposing to take. After getting us to sign the list she put it away and immediately started saying goodbye.

'You've quite forgotten us, Pyotr Petrovich,' she told Belokurov as she gave him her hand. 'Please come and see us – and if Monsieur N— (she mentioned my name) would like to see some admirers of his work and fancies paying us a visit, Mama and I would be really delighted.' I bowed.

When she had driven off Pyotr Petrovich started telling me about her. He said that the girl was of good family and that her name was Lidiya Volchaninov. The estate on which she lived with her mother and sister – like the large village on the other side of the pond –

was called Shelkovka. Her father had once held an important post in Moscow and was a high-ranking civil servant when he died. Although they were very well-off, the Volchaninovs never left their estate, summer or winter. Lidiya taught in their own rural school in Shelkovka, at a monthly salary of twenty-five roubles. She spent nothing else besides this money on herself and was proud of earning her own living.

'An interesting family,' said Belokurov. 'We'll go and visit them one day if you like. They'd be delighted to see you.'

One day after dinner (it was some sort of holiday) we remembered the Volchaninovs and went over to see them at Shelkovka. The mother and her two daughters were at home. Yekaterina Pavlovna, the mother, obviously once very pretty but now plump for her age, sad, short-winded and absent-minded, tried to entertain me with talk about painting. Having learnt from her daughter that I might be coming to see them at Shelkovka she hurriedly mentioned two or three of my landscapes that she had seen at Moscow exhibitions, and now she asked me what I wanted to express in them. Lidiya – or Lida as she was called at home – talked more to Belokurov than to me. Serious and unsmiling, she asked him why he wasn't on the local council and had so far never attended a single meeting.

'It's not right!' she said reproachfully. 'It's not right. You should be ashamed of yourself.'

'That's true, perfectly true,' her mother agreed. 'It's just not right!'

'The whole district is under Balagin's thumb,' Lida

continued, turning to me. 'He himself is chairman of the council, he's handed out all the jobs in the district to his nephews and sons-in-law, and he does just what he likes. We must take a stand. The young people must form a pressure group, but you can see for yourself what our young people are like. You ought to be ashamed of yourself, Pyotr Petrovich!'

While we were discussing the local council, Zhenya, the younger sister, said nothing. She never took part in serious conversations: in that family she wasn't considered grown-up at all – just as if she were a little girl they called her Missy, the name she had given her governess as a child. The whole time she kept looking at me inquisitively and when I was examining the photographs in the album she explained: 'That's Uncle . . . that's my godfather . . .' and she ran her finger over the photographs, touching me with her shoulder like a child, so that I had a close view of her delicate, undeveloped bosom, her slender shoulders, her plait and her slim, tight-belted waist.

We played croquet and tennis, strolled in the garden, drank tea, after which we had a leisurely supper. After that vast, empty colonnaded ballroom I somehow felt at home in that small, cosy house where there were no oleographs on the walls and where the servants were spoken to politely. Thanks to Lida and Missy, everything seemed so pure and youthful: it was all so civilized. Over supper Lida again talked to Belokurov about the council, about Balagin and school libraries. She was a vivacious, sincere girl with strong views. And it was fascinating listening to her, although she said a lot, and in a loud voice – perhaps because that was how she was used to speaking in school. On the other hand my friend Pyotr Petrovich, who still retained the student habit of turning everything into an argument, spoke boringly, listlessly and longwindedly – he was obviously most anxious to appear advanced and clever. He waved his arms about and upset a sauceboat with his sleeve, so that a large pool of gravy formed on the tablecloth. But I was the only one who seemed to notice it.

It was quiet and dark when we returned.

'Good breeding isn't that you don't upset gravy on tablecloths, but that you don't notice when someone else does it,' sighed Belokurov. 'Yes, they're a splendid, cultured family. I'm out of touch with refined people – ever so badly out of touch! Nothing but work, work, work!'

He spoke of all the work involved in being a model farmer. But I thought to myself: what an unpleasant, lazy fellow! Whenever he spoke about anything serious he would laboriously drag out his words with a great deal of 'er's and 'erring'. And he worked as he spoke – slowly, always late, always missing deadlines. I had little confidence in his efficiency, if only because he carried around for weeks on end in his pockets the letters I'd given him to post.

'The hardest thing,' he muttered as he walked beside me, 'is not having your work appreciated by anyone! You get no thanks at all!'

II

I became a regular visitor at the Volchaninovs. Usually I would sit on the bottom step of the terrace, depressed by feelings of dissatisfaction with myself, regretting that my life was passing so quickly, so uninterestingly. I kept thinking how marvellous it would be if I could somehow tear my heart, which felt so heavy, out of my chest. Just then they were talking on the terrace and I could hear the rustle of dresses, the sound of someone turning over pages in a book. I soon became used to Lida receiving the sick and handing out books during the day. Often she would go off to the village with a parasol over her bare head, while in the evenings she would hold forth in a loud voice about councils and schools. Whenever the conversation turned to serious matters, that slim, pretty, invariably severe young lady with her small, finely modelled mouth, would coldly tell me:

'That's of no interest to you.'

I did not appeal to her at all. She did not like me because I was a landscape painter who did not portray the hardships of the common people in my canvases and because – so she thought – I was indifferent to all her deepest beliefs. I remember, when I was once travelling along the shores of Lake Baikal I met a young Buryat girl on horseback, wearing a smock and cotton trousers. I asked her to sell me her pipe, but while we were talking she looked contemptuously at my European face and hat. All of a sudden she became tired of talking and galloped off, uttering wild yells. And in the same way Lida looked down on me, because we were from different worlds. She didn't express her dislike openly, but I could sense it. Sitting on the bottom step of the terrace I felt irritated and told her that dishing out treatment to peasants without being a doctor was a fraud: it was easy enough to play the Good Samaritan when one had five thousand acres of one's own.

But her sister Missy didn't have a care in the world. Like me, she lived a life of complete idleness. The moment she got up in the morning she would take a book and sit reading in a deep armchair on the terrace with her feet barely touching the ground; or she would escape with her book to the lime-tree avenue, or go beyond the gates into the open fields. She would read all day long, eagerly poring over her book and one could only tell from her occasionally tired and glazed look, and her extreme pallor, how taxing this really was for her. When I came she would blush slightly on seeing me, put down her book, look into my face with her big eyes and tell me enthusiastically what had been happening – for example, that the chimney in the servants' quarters had caught fire, or that a workman had hooked a large fish in the pond. On weekdays she usually went around in a brightly coloured blouse and navy blue skirt. We would go for walks together, pick cherries for jam or go boating and whenever she jumped up to reach the cherries or plied the oars her thin, delicate arms showed through her full sleeves. Occasionally, I would sketch while she stood beside me, looking on admiringly.

One Sunday at the end of July I went over to the Volchaninovs at about nine in the morning and I walked through the park, keeping as far as I could away from the house, looking for white mushrooms which were plentiful that summer and putting down markers so that I could return later with Zhenya to pick them. A warm breeze was blowing. I saw Zhenya and her mother, both in bright Sunday dresses, coming back from church. Zhenya was holding onto her hat in the wind. Then I could hear them having breakfast on the terrace.

For a carefree person like myself, forever trying to find an excuse for his perpetual idleness, these Sunday mornings on our estates in summer always had a particular charm. When the green garden, still wet with dew, gleams in the sun and seems to be rejoicing; when there is the scent of mignonette and oleander by the house; when the young people have just returned from church and are having breakfast in the garden; when everyone is dressed so charmingly and is so gay; when you know that all these healthy, well-fed, handsome people will be doing nothing all day long – then one wishes life to be always like that. And these were my thoughts as I walked through the garden, ready to wander just like this, idly and aimlessly, all day, all summer.

Zhenya came out with a basket and she looked as if she knew or sensed she would find me in the garden. We gathered mushrooms and when she asked me something she would go on ahead, so that she could see my face.

'There was a miracle in our village yesterday,' she said. 'That lame Pelageya's been ill the whole year, no doctors or medicine did her any good. But yesterday an old woman recited a spell and she got better.'

'That's nothing much,' I said. 'You shouldn't look for miracles only among the sick and old women. Isn't health a miracle? And life itself? Anything we can't understand is a miracle.'

'But aren't you scared of things you don't understand?'

'No, I face up to phenomena I don't understand boldly and I don't allow myself to be intimidated. I'm on a higher level than them. Man should consider himself superior to lions, tigers, stars – to everything in nature – even those things he doesn't understand and thinks of as miraculous. Otherwise he's not a man but a mouse, afraid of everything.'

Zhenya thought that, as I was an artist, I must know a great deal and could accurately guess what I didn't know. She wanted me to lead her into the realm of the eternal and beautiful, into that loftier world in which, she fancied, I was quite at home. And she spoke to me of God, of immortality, of the miraculous. I refused to admit that I and my imagination would perish for ever after death. 'Yes, people are immortal. Yes, eternal life awaits us,' I replied. And she listened and believed – and she did not ask for proof.

When we were going back to the house she suddenly stopped and said: 'Lida's a remarkable person, isn't she? I love her dearly and I would readily sacrifice my life for her. But tell me,' Zhenya continued, touching my

sleeve with her finger, 'tell me why you're always arguing with her? Why do you get so exasperated?'

'Because she's in the wrong.'

Zhenya shook her head and tears came into her eyes.
'I just don't understand,' she murmured.

Lida had just returned from somewhere and she
stood by the front porch, crop in hand, graceful and
beautiful in the sunlight; she was giving orders to one
of the workmen. Talking very loudly, she hurriedly saw
two or three patients and then, with a preoccupied,
busy look, marched through the rooms, opening one
cupboard after the other, after which she went up to
the attic storey. For a long time they looked for her, to
tell her dinner was ready, and by the time she came
down we were already finishing our soup. I remember
and cherish all these little details and I vividly remember the whole of that day, although it wasn't particularly eventful. After dinner Zhenya lay in a deep
armchair reading, while I sat on the bottom step of the
terrace. We said nothing. The sky was overcast and
a fine drizzle had set in. It was hot, the wind had
long dropped and it seemed the day would never end.
Yekaterina Pavlovna came out onto the terrace with a
fan – she looked half asleep.

'Oh, Mama!' Zhenya said, kissing her hand. 'It's not
healthy sleeping during the day.'

They adored each other. When one went into the
garden, the other would be standing on the terrace
looking towards the trees, calling out: 'Hullo, Zhenya!'
or 'Mama, where are you?' They always prayed together, both shared the same faith and they understood

one another perfectly, even when they said nothing. And they both had the same attitude towards people. Yekaterina Pavlovna also took to me in no time at all and when I didn't appear for two or three days she would send someone over to inquire if I was well. She would also gaze admiringly at my sketches and would rattle away about all the latest news – just as readily as Missy; and she often confided family secrets to me.

She revered her elder daughter. Lida never made up to her and would only discuss serious matters with her. She lived a life apart and for her mother and sister she was godlike, something of an enigma, just like an admiral who never leaves his cabin.

'Our Lida's a remarkable person, isn't she?' her mother would often say.

And now, as the drizzle came down, we talked about Lida.

'She's a remarkable person,' her mother said, adding in a muted, conspiratorial tone as she glanced anxiously over her shoulder: 'You don't find many like her. Only I'm getting rather worried, you know. The school, the dispensaries, books – all that's most commendable, but why go to such extremes? After all, she's twenty-three, it's time she thought seriously about herself. What with all those books and dispensaries her life will be over before she even notices it ... it's time she got married.'

Pale from reading, her hair in disarray, Zhenya raised her head a little, looked at her mother and said as if to herself: 'Mama, everything depends on God's will.'

And once again she buried herself in her book.

Belokurov arrived in his peasant jerkin and embroidered smock. We played croquet and tennis. And then, after dark, we enjoyed a leisurely supper. Again Lida talked about schools and that Balagin, who had the whole district under his thumb. As I left the Volchaninovs that evening I took away with me an impression of a long, idle day – and the sad realization that everything in this world comes to an end, however long it may appear. Zhenya saw us to the gates and, perhaps because she had spent the whole day with me from morning to night, I felt that without her everything was such a bore and I realized how dear this whole charming family was to me. And for the first time that summer I had the urge to paint.

'Tell me, why do you lead such a boring, drab life?' I asked Belokurov as we went back. 'My own life is boring, difficult, monotonous, because I'm an artist. I'm an odd kind of chap; since I was young I've been plagued by feelings of hatred, by frustration with myself, by lack of belief in my work. I've always been poor, I'm a vagrant. But as for you – you're a normal, healthy man, a landowner, a squire. So why do you lead such a boring life? Why do you take so little from it? For instance, why have you never fallen in love with Lida or Zhenya?'

'You're forgetting that I love another woman,' Belokurov replied.

He was talking of his companion Lyubov Ivanovna, who lived in the cottage with him. Every day I saw that plump, podgy, self-important woman – rather like a fattened goose – strolling around the garden in a traditional beaded folk costume, always carrying a parasol. The servants were always calling her in for a meal, or for tea. Three years ago she had rented one of the holiday cottages and had simply stayed on to live with Belokurov – for ever, it seemed. She was about ten years older than him and ruled him with a rod of iron – so much so that he had to ask permission whenever he wanted to go somewhere. She often sobbed in a deep, masculine voice and then I would send word that I would move out of the flat if she didn't stop. And stop she did.

When we were back Belokurov sat on my couch with a pensive frown, while I paced the room, feeling a gentle excitement, as if I were in love. I wanted to talk about the Volchaninovs.

'Lida could only fall in love with a council worker who is as devoted as she is to hospitals and schools,' I said. 'Oh, for a girl like her one would not only do welfare work but even wear out a pair of iron boots, like the girl in the fairy-tale! And there's Missy. Isn't she charming, this Missy!'

Belokurov embarked on a long-winded discussion about the malady of the age – pessimism – dragging out those 'er's. He spoke confidently and his tone suggested that I was quarrelling with him. Hundreds of miles of bleak, monotonous, scorched steppe can never be so utterly depressing as someone who just sits and chatters away – and you have no idea when he's going to leave you in peace.

'Pessimism or optimism have nothing to do with it,'

I said, irritably. 'The point is, ninety-nine people out of a hundred have no brains.'

Belokurov took this personally and left in a huff.

III

'The prince is staying in Malozyomovo and sends his regards,' Lida told her mother. She had just come in from somewhere and was removing her gloves. 'He had many interesting things to tell us . . . He promised to raise the question of a clinic for Malozyomovo with the council again, but stressed that there was little hope.' Turning to me she said: 'I'm sorry, I keep forgetting that kind of thing's of no interest to you.'

This really got my back up.

'Why isn't it interesting?' I asked, shrugging my shoulders. 'You don't want to know my opinion, but I assure you that the question interests me a great deal.'

'Really?'

'Yes, really. In my opinion they don't need a clinic at Malozyomovo.'

My irritation was infectious. She looked at me, screwed up her eyes and asked: 'What do they need then? Landscape paintings?'

'They don't need landscapes either. They don't need anything.'

She finished taking off her gloves and unfolded the paper that had just been collected from the post office. A minute later she said quietly, as if trying to control herself: 'Last week Anna died in childbirth. If there'd been a clinic near her she'd be alive now. And I really do think that our fine gentlemen landscape painters should have some opinions on that score.'

'I have very definite views on that score, I assure you,' I replied – and she hid behind her paper as if she didn't want to listen. 'To my mind, with things as they are, clinics, schools, libraries, dispensaries only serve to enslave people. The peasants are weighed down by a great chain and instead of breaking this chain you're only adding new links – that's what I think.'

She raised her eyes and smiled ironically as I continued, trying to catch the main thread of my argument:

'What matters is not Anna dying in childbirth, but that all these peasant Annas, Mavras and Pelageyas toil away from dawn to dusk and that this unremitting labour makes them ill. All their lives they go in fear and trembling for their sick and hungry children, dreading death and illness. All their lives they're being treated for some illness. They fade away before their time and die in filth and stench. And as their children grow up it's the same old story. And so the centuries pass and untold millions of people live worse than animals, wondering where their next meal will come from, hounded by constant fear. The whole horror of their situation is that they have no time to think of their souls, no time to remember that they were created in the image and likeness of their Creator. Famine, irrational fears, unceasing toil – these are like avalanches, blocking all paths to spiritual activity, which is precisely what distinguishes man from beast and makes life worth living. You come to their aid with hospitals and schools, but this doesn't free them from their shackles: on the contrary, you enslave them even more since, by introducing fresh prejudices you increase the number of their needs – not to mention the fact that they have to pay the council for their plasters and books – and so they have to slave away even harder.'

'I'm not going to argue with you,' Lida said, putting down her paper. 'I've heard it all before. But I'll say one thing: you can't just sit twiddling your thumbs. True, we're not the saviours of humanity and perhaps we make lots of mistakes, but we are doing what we can and we are right. The loftiest, most sacred task for any civilized man is to serve his neighbours – and we try to serve them as best we can. You don't like it, but there's no pleasing everyone.'

'True, Lida, that's true,' her mother said.

In Lida's presence she was always rather timid, glancing nervously at her when she spoke and afraid of saying something superfluous or irrelevant. And she never contradicted her:

'True, Lida, that's true,' she always agreed.

'Teaching peasants to read and write, books full of wretched maxims and sayings, clinics, cannot reduce either ignorance or the death-rate, just as the light from your windows cannot illuminate this huge garden,' I said. 'You contribute nothing by meddling in these people's lives, you're simply creating new needs and even more reasons for them to slave away.'

'Oh, God! Surely something has to be done,' Lida said irritably and from her tone I gathered that she considered my arguments trivial and beneath contempt.

'The people must be freed from heavy physical work,' I said. 'We must lighten their yoke, they must have breathing-space, so that they don't have to spend all their lives at the stove, wash-tub and in the fields, so that they have time to think of their souls, of God and thus develop their spiritual lives. Man's true vocation is the life of the spirit, the constant search for truth, for the meaning of life. Liberate them from this rough, brutish labour, let them feel they are free – then you'll see what a farce these dispensaries and books really are. Once a man recognizes his true vocation, only religion, science, art can satisfy him – not all this nonsense of yours.'

'Free them from labour!' Lida laughed. 'Can that be possible?'

'It can. You must take some of their labour on your own shoulders. If all of us town and country dwellers unanimously agreed to divide among ourselves the labour that is normally expended by humanity on the satisfaction of its physical needs, then each of us would probably have to work no more than two or three hours a day. Just imagine if all of us, rich and poor, worked only two or three hours a day and had the rest of the time to ourselves. Imagine if we invented labour-saving machines and tried to reduce our needs to the absolute minimum so as to be less dependent on our bodies and to be able to work even less. We would harden ourselves and our children so that they would no longer fear hunger or cold. We wouldn't be constantly worrying about their health, unlike Anna, Mavra and Pelageya. Imagine if we no longer doctored ourselves, didn't maintain dispensaries, tobacco factories, distilleries – how much more leisure time we'd finally have at our disposal! All of us, working together, would be able to devote our leisure to science and art. Just as peasants sometimes mend roads, working as a community, so all of us, as one big community, would search for the truth and the meaning of life: and the truth would be discovered very quickly, man would rid himself of this constant, agonizing, oppressive fear of death – and even from death itself – of that I'm convinced.'

'But you're contradicting yourself,' Lida said. 'You keep going on about science and art, yet you yourself reject literacy.'

'The kind of literacy, when a man has nothing else to read except pub signs and sometimes books he doesn't understand, has been with us since Ryurik's time. Gogol's Petrushka's been able to read for absolutely ages, whereas our villages are exactly the same as they were in Ryurik's time. It isn't literacy that we need, but freedom to develop our spiritual faculties as widely as possible. We don't need schools – we need universities.'

'And you reject medicine as well?'

'Yes. Medicine might be necessary for the study of diseases as natural phenomena, but not for their treatment. If you want to cure people you shouldn't treat the illness but its cause. Take away the main cause – physical labour – and there won't be any more diseases. I don't recognize the healing arts,' I continued excitedly. 'Genuine science and art don't strive towards temporary, personal ends, but towards the universal and eternal: they seek truth and the meaning of life, they seek God, the soul. But if you reduce them to the level of everyday needs, to the mundane, to dispensaries and libraries, they only complicate life and make it more difficult. We have loads of doctors, pharmacists, lawyers, lots of people who can read and write, but there's a complete lack of biologists, mathematicians, philosophers and poets. One's entire intellect, one's entire spiritual energy has been used up satisfying transient, temporary needs. Scholars, writers and artists are working away – thanks to them life's comforts increase with every day. Our physical needs multiply, whereas the truth is still far, far off and man still remains the most predatory and filthy of animals and everything conspires towards the larger part of mankind degenerating and losing its vitality. In such conditions an artist's life has no meaning and the more talented he is the stranger and more incomprehensible his role, since, on closer inspection, it turns out that, by supporting the existing order, he's working for the amusement of this rapacious, filthy animal. I don't want to work . . . and I *shan't*! I don't need a thing, the whole world can go to hell!'

'Missy dear, you'd better leave the room,' Lida told her sister, evidently finding my words harmful for such a young girl.

Zhenya sadly looked at her sister and mother and went out.

'People who want to justify their own indifference usually come out with such charming things,' Lida said. 'Rejecting hospitals and schools is easier than healing people or teaching.'

'That's true, Lida, that's true,' her mother agreed.

'Now you're threatening to give up working,' Lida continued. 'It's obvious you value your painting very highly! But let's stop arguing. We'll never see eye to eye, since I value the most imperfect of these libraries or dispensaries – of which you spoke so contemptuously just now – more highly than all the landscapes in the world.' Turning to her mother she immediately continued in an entirely different tone of voice: 'The prince has grown much thinner, he's changed dramatically since he was last with us. They're sending him to Vichy.'

She told her mother about the prince to avoid talking to me. Her face was burning and to hide her agitation she bent low over the table as if she were short-sighted, and pretended to be reading the paper. My company was disagreeable for them. I said goodbye and went home.

IV

It was quiet outside. The village on the far side of the pond was already asleep. Not a single light was visible, only the pale reflections of the stars faintly glimmered on the water. Zhenya stood motionless at the gates with the lions, waiting to see me off.

'Everyone's asleep in the village,' I told her, trying to make out her face in the gloom – and I saw those dark, mournful eyes fixed on me. 'The innkeeper and horse thieves are peacefully sleeping, while we respectable people quarrel and annoy one another.'

It was a sad August night – sad because there was already a breath of autumn in the air. The moon was rising, veiled by a crimson cloud and casting a dim light on the road and the dark fields of winter corn along its sides. There were many shooting stars. Zhenya walked along the road by my side, trying not to see the shooting stars, which frightened her for some reason.

'I think you're right,' she said, trembling from the damp night air. 'If people would only work together, if they could give themselves up to the life of the spirit they would soon know everything.'

'Of course, we're superior beings and if in fact we did recognize the full power of human genius and lived only for some higher end, then in the long run we'd all come to be like gods. But that will never happen – mankind will degenerate and not a trace of genius will remain.'

When we could no longer see the gates Zhenya stopped and hurriedly shook hands with me.

'Good night,' she said with a shudder. Only a thin blouse covered her shoulders and she huddled up from the cold. 'Please come tomorrow!'

I was horrified at the prospect of being left alone and felt agitated and unhappy with myself and others. And I too tried not to look at the shooting stars.

'Please stay a little longer,' I said. 'Please do!'

I loved Zhenya. I loved her – perhaps – for meeting me and seeing me off, for looking so tenderly and admiringly at me. Her pale face, her slender neck, her frailty, her idleness, her books – they were so moving

36

in their beauty! And what about her mind? I suspected that she was extremely intelligent. The breadth of her views enchanted me, perhaps because she thought differently from the severe, pretty Lida, who disliked me. Zhenya liked me as an artist. I had won her heart with my talent and I longed to paint for her alone. I dreamt of her as my little queen who would hold sway with me over these trees, fields, this mist, sunset, over this exquisite, magical nature where I had so far felt hopelessly lonely and unwanted.

'Please stay a little longer,' I asked. 'Please stay!'

I took off my coat and covered her chilled shoulders. Afraid that she might look silly and unattractive in a man's coat, she threw it off – and then I embraced her and started showering her face, shoulders and arms with kisses.

'Till tomorrow!' she cried.

For about two minutes after that I could hear her running. I didn't feel like going home and I had no reason for going there anyway. I stood and reflected for a moment and then slowly made my way back to have another look at that dear, innocent old house that seemed to be staring at me with its attic windows as if they were all-comprehending eyes. I walked past the terrace and sat down on a bench in the darkness under the old elm by the tennis court. In the windows of the attic storey where she slept a bright light suddenly shone, turning soft green when the lamp was covered with a shade. Shadows stirred. I was full of tenderness, calm and contentment – contentment because I had let myself be carried away and had fallen in love. And at the same time I was troubled by the thought that only a few steps away Lida lived in one of the rooms of that house – Lida, who disliked and possibly even hated me. I sat waiting for Zhenya to come out. I listened hard and people seemed to be talking in the attic storey.

About an hour passed. The green light went out and the shadows vanished. The moon stood high now over the house and illuminated the sleeping garden, the paths. Dahlias and roses in the flowerbeds in front of the house were clearly visible and all of them seemed the same colour. It became very cold. I left the garden, picked up my coat from the path and unhurriedly made my way home.

Next day, when I arrived at the Volchaninovs after dinner, the French windows into the garden were wide open. I sat for a while on the terrace, expecting Zhenya to appear any minute behind the flowerbed by the tennis court, or on one of the avenues – or her voice to come from one of the rooms. Then I went through the drawing-room and dining-room. There wasn't a soul about. From the dining-room I walked down a long corridor to the hall and back. In the corridor there were several doors and through one of them I could hear Lida's voice.

'God sent a crow . . .' she was saying in a loud, deliberate voice – probably dictating – 'God sent a crow a piece of cheese . . . Who's there?' she suddenly called out, hearing my footsteps.

'It's me.'

'Oh, I'm sorry, but I can't come out now. I'm busy with Dasha.'

'Is Yekaterina Pavlovna in the garden?'

'No. She went this morning with my sister to her aunt's in Penza. This winter they'll probably go abroad,' she added after a pause.

'Go-od se-ent a crow a pi-iece of che-eese. Have you written that down?'

I went into the hall and stared vacantly at the pond and the village. And I could hear her voice: 'A pi-iece of che-eese . . . Go-od sent the crow . . .'

And I left the grounds the same way I had first come: from the courtyard into the garden, past the house, then along the lime-tree avenue. Here a boy caught up with me and handed me a note.

'I've told my sister everything and she insists we break up,' I read. 'I could never upset her by disobeying. May God grant you happiness. I'm sorry. If you only knew how bitterly Mama and I are crying.'

Then came the dark fir avenue, the broken-down fence. On that same field where once I had seen the flowering rye and heard the quails calling, cows and hobbled horses were now grazing. Here and there on the hills were the bright green patches of winter corn. A sober, humdrum mood came over me and I felt ashamed of all I had said at the Volchaninovs. And I was as bored as ever with life. When I got home I packed and left for St Petersburg that same evening.

I never saw the Volchaninovs again. Not long ago, however, I met Belokurov on the train when I was travelling to the Crimea. He was still wearing that peasant jerkin and embroidered smock, and when I inquired about his health he replied that he was well –

thank you very much! We started talking. He had sold his estate and bought a smaller one in Lyubov Ivanovna's name. He told me Lida was still living in Shelkovka and teaching in the school. Gradually she'd managed to gather around her a circle of congenial spirits, a pressure group, and at the last local election they'd 'blackballed' Balagin, who up to then had his hands on the whole district. As for Zhenya, Belokurov only told me that she wasn't living at home and that he didn't know where she was.

I'm already beginning to forget that old house with the mezzanine and only occasionally, when I'm painting or reading, do I suddenly remember – for no apparent reason – that green light in the window; or the sound of my footsteps as I walked home across the fields at night, in love, rubbing my hands in the cold. And even more rarely, when I am sad at heart and afflicted with loneliness, do I have dim memories. And gradually I come to feel that I haven't been forgotten either, that she is waiting for me and that we'll meet again . . .

Missy, where are you?

A Visit to Friends

(A STORY)

A letter arrived one morning.

Dear Misha,
You've completely forgotten us, please come and visit us
soon, we so want to see you. Come today. We beg you, dear
sir, on bended knees! Show us your radiant eyes!
Can't wait to see you,
Ta and Va

The letter was from Tatyana Alekseyevna Losev, who
had been called 'Ta' for short when Podgorin was
staying at Kuzminki ten or twelve years ago. But who
was this 'Va'? Podgorin recalled the long conversations,
the gay laughter, the love affairs, the evening walks and
that whole array of girls and young women who had
once lived at Kuzminki and in the neighbourhood.
And he remembered that open, lively, clever face with
freckles that matched chestnut hair so well – this was
Varvara Pavlovna, Tatyana's friend. Varvara Pavlovna
had taken a degree in medicine and was working at a
factory somewhere beyond Tula. Evidently she had
come to stay at Kuzminki now.

'Dear Va!' thought Podgorin, surrendering himself to memories. 'What a wonderful girl!'

Tatyana, Varvara and himself were all about the same age. But he had been a mere student then and they were already marriageable girls – in their eyes he was just a boy. And now, even though he had become a lawyer and had started to go grey, all of them still treated him like a youngster, saying that he had no experience of life yet.

He was very fond of them, but more as a pleasant memory than in actuality, it seemed. He knew little about their present life, which was strange and alien to him. And this brief, playful letter too was something quite foreign to him and had most probably been written after much time and effort. When Tatyana wrote it her husband Sergey Sergeich was doubtlessly standing behind her. She had been given Kuzminki as her dowry only six years before, but this same Sergey Sergeich had already reduced the estate to bankruptcy. Each time a bank or mortgage payment became due they would now turn to Podgorin for legal advice. Moreover, they had twice asked him to lend them money. So it was obvious that they either wanted advice or a loan from him now.

He no longer felt so attracted to Kuzminki as in the past. It was such a miserable place. That laughter and rushing around, those cheerful carefree faces, those rendezvous on quiet moonlit nights – all this had gone. Most important, though, they weren't in the flush of youth any more. Probably it enchanted him only as a memory, nothing else. Besides Ta and Va, there was someone called 'Na', Tatyana's sister Nadezhda, whom half-joking, half-seriously they had called his fiancée. He had seen her grow up and everyone expected him to marry her. He had loved her once and was going to propose. But there she was, twenty-three now, and he still hadn't married her.

'Strange it should turn out like this,' he mused as he reread the letter in embarrassment. 'But I can't *not* go, they'd be offended.'

His long absence from the Losevs lay like a heavy weight on his conscience. After pacing his room and reflecting at length, he made a great effort of will and decided to go and visit them for about three days and so discharge his duty. Then he could feel free and relaxed – at least until the following summer. After lunch, as he prepared to leave for the Brest Station, he told his servants that he would be back in three days.

It was two hours by train from Moscow to Kuzminki, then a twenty-minute carriage drive from the station, from which he could see Tatyana's wood and those three tall, narrow holiday villas that Losev (he had entered upon some business enterprise in the first years of his marriage) had started building but had never finished. He had been ruined by these holiday villas, by various business projects, by frequent trips to Moscow, where he used to lunch at the Slav Fair and dine at the Hermitage, ending up in Little Bronny Street or at a gipsy haunt named Knacker's Yard, calling this 'having a fling'. Podgorin liked a drink himself – sometimes quite a lot – and he associated with women indiscriminately, but in a cool, lethargic way, without deriving any pleasure. It sickened him when others gave themselves up to these pleasures with such zest. He didn't understand or like men who could feel more free and easy at the Knacker's Yard than at home with a respectable woman, and he felt that any kind of promiscuity stuck to them like burrs. He didn't care for Losev, considering him a boring, lazy, old bungler and more than once had found his company rather repulsive.

Just past the wood, Sergey Sergeich and Nadezhda met him.

'My dear fellow, why have you forgotten us?' Sergey Sergeich asked, kissing him three times and then putting both arms round his waist. 'You don't feel affection for us any more, old chap.'

He had coarse features, a fat nose and a thin, light-brown beard. He combed his hair to one side to make himself look like a typical simple Russian. When he spoke he breathed right into your face and when he wasn't speaking he'd breathe heavily through the nose. He was embarrassed by his plumpness and inordinately replete appearance and would keep thrusting out his chest to breathe more easily, which made him look pompous.

In comparison, his sister-in-law Nadezhda seemed ethereal. She was very fair, pale-faced and slim, with kind, loving eyes. Podgorin couldn't judge as to her beauty, since he'd known her since she was a child and grown used to the way she looked. Now she was wearing a white, open-necked dress and the sight of that long, white bare neck was new to him and not altogether pleasant.

'My sister and I have been waiting for you since morning,' she said. 'Varvara's here and she's been expecting you, too.'

She took his arm and suddenly laughed for no reason, uttering a faint cry of joy as if some thought had unexpectedly cast a spell over her. The fields of flowering rye, motionless in the quiet air, the sunlit wood – they were so beautiful. Nadezhda seemed to notice these things only now, as she walked at Podgorin's side.

'I'll be staying about three days,' he told her. 'I'm sorry, but I just couldn't get away from Moscow any earlier.'

'That's not very nice at all, you've forgotten we exist!' Sergey Sergeich said, reproaching him good-humouredly. '*Jamais de ma vie!*' he suddenly added, snapping his fingers. He had this habit of suddenly blurting out some irrelevance, snapping his fingers in the process. He was always mimicking someone: if he rolled his eyes, or nonchalantly tossed his hair back, or adopted a dramatic pose, that meant he had been to the theatre the night before, or to some dinner with speeches. Now he took short steps as he walked, like an old gout-ridden man, and without bending his knees – he was most likely imitating someone.

'Do you know, Tanya wouldn't believe you'd come,' Nadezhda said. 'But Varvara and I had a funny feeling about it. I somehow *knew* you'd be on that train.'

'*Jamais de ma vie!*' Sergey Sergeich repeated.

The ladies were waiting for them on the garden terrace. Ten years ago Podgorin – then a poor student – had given Nadezhda coaching in maths and history

45

in exchange for board and lodging. Varvara, who was studying medicine at the time, happened to be taking Latin lessons from him. As for Tatyana, already a beautiful mature girl then, she could think of nothing but love. All she had desired was love and happiness and she would yearn for them, forever waiting for the husband she dreamed of night and day. Past thirty now, she was just as beautiful and attractive as ever, in her loose-fitting peignoir and with those plump, white arms. Her only thought was for her husband and two little girls. Although she was talking and smiling now, her expression revealed that she was preoccupied with other matters. She was still guarding her love and her rights to that love and was always on the alert, ready to attack any enemy who might want to take her husband and children away from her. Her love was very strong and she felt that it was reciprocated, but jealousy and fear for her children were a constant torment and prevented her from being happy.

After the noisy reunion on the terrace, everyone except Sergey Sergeich went to Tatyana's room. The sun's rays did not penetrate the lowered blinds and it was so gloomy there that all the roses in a large bunch looked the same colour. They made Podgorin sit down in an old armchair by the window; Nadezhda sat on a low stool at his feet. Besides the kindly reproaches, the jokes and laughter that reminded him so clearly of the past, he knew he could expect an unpleasant conversation about promissory notes and mortgages. It couldn't be avoided, so he thought that it might be best to get down to business there and then without delaying matters, to get it over and done with and then go out into the garden, into fresh air.

'Shall we discuss business first?' he said. 'What's new here in Kuzminki? Is something rotten in the state of Denmark?'

'Kuzminki is in a bad way,' Tatyana replied, sadly sighing. 'Things are so bad it's hard to imagine they could be any worse.' She paced the room, highly agitated. 'Our estate's for sale, the auction's on 7 August. Everywhere there's advertisements, and buyers come here – they walk through the house, looking . . . Now anyone has the right to go into my room and look round. That may be legal, but it's humiliating for me and deeply insulting. We've no funds – and there's nowhere left to borrow any from. Briefly, it's shocking!'

She stopped in the middle of the room, the tears trickling from her eyes, and her voice trembled as she went on, 'I swear, I swear by all that's holy, by my children's happiness, I can't live without Kuzminki! I was born here, it's my home. If they take it away from me I shall never get over it, I'll die of despair.'

'I think you're rather looking on the black side,' Podgorin said. 'Everything will turn out all right. Your husband will get a job, you'll settle down again, lead a new life . . .'

'How *can* you say that!' Tatyana shouted. Now she looked very beautiful and aggressive. She was ready to fall on the enemy who wanted to take her husband, children and home away from her, and this was expressed with particular intensity in her face and whole figure. 'A new life! I ask you! Sergey Sergeich's been busy applying for jobs and they've promised him a position as tax inspector somewhere near Ufa or Perm – or thereabouts. I'm ready to go anywhere. Siberia even. I'm prepared to live there ten, twenty years, but I must be certain that sooner or later I'll return to Kuzminki. I can't live without Kuzminki. I can't, and I won't!' She shouted and stamped her foot.

'Misha, you're a lawyer,' Varvara said, 'you know all the tricks and it's your job to advise us what to do.'

There was only one fair and reasonable answer to this, that there was nothing anyone could do, but Podgorin could not bring himself to say it outright.

'I'll . . . have a think about it,' he mumbled indecisively. 'I'll have a think about it . . .'

He was really two different persons. As a lawyer he had to deal with some very ugly cases. In court and with clients he behaved arrogantly and always expressed his opinion bluntly and curtly. He was used to crudely living it up with his friends. But in his private, intimate life he displayed uncommon tact with people close to him or with very old friends. He was shy and sensitive and tended to beat about the bush. One tear, one sidelong glance, a lie or even a rude gesture was enough to make him wince and lose his nerve. Now that Nadezhda was sitting at his feet he disliked her bare neck. It palled on him and even made him feel like going home. A year ago he had happened to bump into Sergey Sergeich at a certain Madame's place in Little Bronny Street and he now felt awkward in Tatyana's company, as if *he* had been the unfaithful one. And this conversation about Kuzminki put him in the most dreadful difficulties. He was used to having ticklish, unpleasant questions decided by judge or jury, or by some legal clause, but faced with a problem that he personally had to solve he was all at sea.

'You're our friend, Misha. We all love you as if you were one of the family,' Tatyana continued. 'And I'll tell you quite candidly: all our hopes rest in you. For heaven's sake, tell us what to do. Perhaps we could write somewhere for help? Perhaps it's not too late to put the estate in Nadezhda's or Varvara's name? What shall we do?'

'Please save us, Misha, *please*,' Varvara said, lighting a cigarette. 'You were always so clever. You haven't seen much of life, you're not very experienced, but you have a fine brain. You'll help Tatyana. I know you will.'

'I must think about it ... perhaps I can come up with something.'

They went for a walk in the garden, then in the fields. Sergey Sergeich went too. He took Podgorin's arm and led him on ahead of the others, evidently intending to discuss something with him – probably the trouble he was in. Walking with Sergey Sergeich and talking to him were an ordeal too. He kept kissing him – always three kisses at a time – took Podgorin's arm, put his own arm round his waist and breathed into his face. He seemed covered with sweet glue that would stick to you if he came close. And that look in his eyes which showed that he wanted something from Podgorin, that he was about to ask him for it, was really quite distressing – it was like having a revolver aimed at you.

The sun had set and it was growing dark. Green and red lights appeared here and there along the railway line. Varvara stopped and as she looked at the lights she started reciting:

> The line runs straight, unswerving,
> Through narrow cuttings,
> Passing posts, crossing bridges,
> While all along the verges,
> Lie buried so many Russian workers!

'How does it go on? Heavens, I've forgotten!'

> In scorching heat, in winter's icy blasts,
> We laboured with backs bent low.

She recited in a magnificent deep voice, with great feeling. Her face flushed brightly, her eyes filled with tears. This was the Varvara that used to be, Varvara the university student, and as he listened Podgorin thought of the past and recalled his student days, when he too knew much fine poetry by heart and loved to recite it.

> He still has not bowed his hunched back
> He's gloomily silent as before . . .

But Varvara could remember no more. She fell silent and smiled weakly, limply. After the recitation those green and red lights seemed sad.

'Oh, I've forgotten it!'

But Podgorin suddenly remembered the lines – somehow they had stuck in his memory from student days and he recited in a soft undertone,

> The Russian worker has suffered enough,
> In building this railway line.
> He will survive to build himself
> A broad bright highway
> By the sweat of his brow . . .
> Only the pity is . . .

'"The pity is,"' Varvara interrupted as she remembered the lines,

> that neither you nor I
> Will ever live to see that wonderful day.

She laughed and slapped him on the shoulder.

They went back to the house and sat down to supper. Sergey Sergeich nonchalantly stuck a corner of his serviette into his collar, imitating someone or other. 'Let's have a drink,' he said, pouring some vodka for himself and Podgorin. 'In our time, we students could hold our drink, we were fine speakers and men of action. I drink your health, old man. So why don't you drink to a stupid old idealist and wish that he will die an idealist? Can the leopard change its spots?'

Throughout supper Tatyana kept looking tenderly and jealously at her husband, anxious lest he ate or drank something that wasn't good for him. She felt that he had been spoilt by women and exhausted by them, and although this was something that appealed to her, it still distressed her. Varvara and Nadezhda also had a soft spot for him and it was obvious from the worried glances they gave him that they were scared he might suddenly get up and leave them. When he wanted to pour himself a second glass Varvara looked angry and said, 'You're poisoning yourself, Sergey Sergeich. You're a highly strung, impressionable man – you could easily become an alcoholic. Tatyana, tell him to remove that vodka.'

On the whole Sergey Sergeich had great success with women. They loved his height, his powerful build, his strong features, his idleness and his tribulations. They said that his extravagance stemmed only from extreme kindness, that he was impractical because he was an idealist. He was honest and high-principled. His inability to adapt to people or circumstances explained why he owned nothing and didn't have a steady job. They trusted him implicitly, idolized him and spoilt him with their adulation, so that he himself came to believe that he really was idealistic, impractical, honest and upright, and that he was head and shoulders above these women.

'Well, don't you have something good to say about my little girls?' Tatyana asked as she looked lovingly at her two daughters – healthy, well-fed and like two fat buns – as she heaped rice on their plates. 'Just take a good look at them. They say all mothers can never speak ill of their children. But I do assure you I'm not at all biased. My little girls are quite remarkable. Especially the elder.'

Podgorin smiled at her and the girls and thought it strange that this healthy, young, intelligent woman, essentially such a strong and complex organism, could waste all her energy, all her strength, on such uncomplicated trivial work as running a home which was well managed anyway.

'Perhaps she knows best,' he thought. 'But it's so boring, so stupid!'

> Before he had time to groan
> A bear came and knocked him prone,

Sergey Sergeich said, snapping his fingers.

They finished their supper. Tatyana and Varvara made Podgorin sit down on a sofa in the drawing-room and, in hushed voices, talked about business again.

'We must save Sergey Sergeich,' Varvara said, 'it's our moral duty. He has his weaknesses, he's not thrifty, he doesn't put anything away for a rainy day, but that's only because he's so kind and generous. He's just a child, really. Give him a million and within a month there'd be nothing left, he'd have given it all away.'

'Yes, that's so true,' Tatyana said and tears rolled down her cheeks. 'I've had a hard time with him, but I must admit he's a wonderful person.'

Both Tatyana and Varvara couldn't help indulging in a little cruelty, telling Podgorin reproachfully, 'Your generation, though, Misha, isn't up to much!'

'What's all this talk about generations?' Podgorin wondered. 'Surely Sergey Sergeich's no more than six years older than me?'

'Life's not easy,' Varvara sighed. 'You're always threatened with losses of some kind. First they want to take your estate away from you, or someone near and dear falls ill and you're afraid he might die. And so it goes on, day after day. But what can one do, my friends? We must submit to a Higher Power without complaining, we must remember that nothing in this world is accidental, everything has its final purpose. Now you, Misha, know little of life, you haven't suffered much and you'll laugh at me. Go ahead and laugh, but I'm going to tell you what I think. When I was passing through a stage of deepest anxiety I experienced second sight on several occasions and this completely transformed my outlook. Now I know that nothing is contingent, everything that happens in life is necessary.'

How different this Varvara was, grey-haired now, and corseted, with her fashionable long-sleeved dress – this Varvara twisting a cigarette between long, thin, trembling fingers – this Varvara so prone to mysticism – this Varvara with such a lifeless, monotonous voice. How different she was from Varvara the medical student, that cheerful, boisterous, adventurous girl with the red hair!

'Where has it all vanished to?' Podgorin wondered, bored with listening to her. 'Sing us a song, Va,' he asked to put a stop to that conversation about second sight. 'You used to have a lovely voice.'

'That's all long ago, Misha.'

'Well, recite some more Nekrasov.'

'I've forgotten it all. Those lines I recited just now I happened to remember.'

Despite the corset and long sleeves she was obviously short of money and had difficulty making ends meet at that factory beyond Tula. It was obvious she'd been overworking. That heavy, monotonous work, that perpetual interfering with other people's business and worrying about them – all this had taken its toll and had aged her. As he looked at that sad face whose freshness had faded, Podgorin concluded that in reality it was *she* who needed help, not Kuzminki or that Sergey Sergeich she was fussing about so much.

Higher education, being a doctor, didn't seem to have had any effect on the woman in her. Just like Tatyana, she loved weddings, births, christenings, interminable conversations about children. She loved spine-chilling stories with happy endings. In newspapers she only read articles about fires, floods and important ceremonies. She longed for Podgorin to propose to Nadezhda – she would have shed tears of emotion if that were to happen.

He didn't know whether it was by chance or Varvara's doing, but Podgorin found himself alone with Nadezhda. However, the mere suspicion that he was being watched, that they wanted something from him, disturbed and inhibited him. In Nadezhda's company he felt as if they had both been put in a cage together.

'Let's go into the garden,' she said.

They went out – he feeling discontented and annoyed that he didn't know what to say, she overjoyed, proud to be near him, and obviously delighted that he was going to spend another three days with them. And perhaps she was filled with sweet fancies and hopes. He didn't know if she loved him, but he did know that she had grown used to him, that she had long been attached to him, that she considered him her teacher, that she was now experiencing the same kind of feelings as her sister Tatyana once had: all she could think of was love, of marrying as soon as possible and having a husband, children, her own place. She had still preserved that readiness for friendship which is usually so strong in children and it was highly probable that she felt for Podgorin and respected him as a friend and that she wasn't in love with *him*, but with her dreams of a husband and children.

'It's getting dark,' he said.

'Yes, the moon rises late now.'

They kept to the same path, near the house. Podgorin didn't want to go deep into the garden – it was dark there and he would have to take Nadezhda by the arm and stay very close to her. Shadows were moving on the terrace and he felt that Tatyana and Varvara were watching him.

'I must ask your advice,' Nadezhda said, stopping. 'If Kuzminki is sold, Sergey Sergeich will leave and get a job and there's no doubt that our lives will be completely changed. I shan't go with my sister, we'll part, because I don't want to be a burden on her family. I'll take a job somewhere in Moscow. I'll earn some money and help Tatyana and her husband. You *will* give me some advice, won't you?'

Quite unaccustomed to any kind of hard work, now she was inspired at the thought of an independent, working life and making plans for the future – this was written all over her face. A life where she would be working and helping others struck her as so beautifully poetic. When he saw that pale face and dark eyebrows so close he remembered what an intelligent, keen pupil she had been, with such fine qualities, a joy to teach. Now she probably wasn't simply a young lady in search of a husband, but an intelligent, decent girl, gentle and soft-hearted, who could be moulded like wax into anything one wished. In the right surroundings she might become a truly wonderful woman!

'Well, why *don't* I marry her then?' Podgorin thought. But he immediately took fright at this idea and went off towards the house. Tatyana was sitting at the grand piano in the drawing-room and her playing conjured up bright pictures of the past, when people had played, sung and danced in that room until late at night, with the windows open and birds singing too in the garden and beyond the river. Podgorin cheered up, became playful, danced with Nadezhda and Varvara, and then sang. He was hampered by a corn on one foot and asked if he could wear Sergey Sergeich's slippers. Strangely, he felt at home, like one of the family, and the thought 'a typical brother-in-law' flashed through his mind. His spirits rose even higher. Looking at him the others livened up and grew cheerful, as if they had recaptured their youth. Everyone's face was radiant with hope: Kuzminki was saved! It was all so very simple in fact. They only had to think of a plan, rummage around in law books, or see that Podgorin married Nadezhda. And that little romance was going well, by all appearances. Pink, happy, her eyes brimming with tears in anticipation of something quite out of the ordinary, Nadezhda whirled round in the dance and her white dress billowed, revealing her small pretty legs in flesh-coloured stockings. Absolutely delighted, Varvara took Podgorin's arm and told him quietly and meaningly, 'Misha, don't run away from happiness. Grasp it while you can. If you wait too long you'll be running when it's too late to catch it.'

Podgorin wanted to make promises, to reassure her and even he began to believe that Kuzminki was saved – it was really so easy.

'"And thou shalt be que-een of the world",' he sang, striking a pose. But suddenly he was conscious that there was nothing he could do for these people, absolutely nothing, and he stopped singing and looked guilty.

Then he sat silently in one corner, legs tucked under him, wearing slippers belonging to someone else.

As they watched him the others understood that nothing could be done and they too fell silent. The piano was closed. Everyone noticed that it was late – it was time for bed – and Tatyana put out the large lamp in the drawing-room.

A bed was made up for Podgorin in the same little outhouse where he had stayed in the past. Sergey Sergeich went with him to wish him goodnight, holding a candle high above his head, although the moon had risen and it was bright. They walked down a path with lilac bushes on either side and the gravel crunched underfoot.

Before he had time to groan
A bear came and knocked him prone,

Sergey Sergeich said.

Podgorin felt that he'd heard those lines a thousand times, he was sick and tired of them! When they reached the outhouse, Sergey Sergeich drew a bottle and two glasses from his loose jacket and put them on the table.

'Brandy,' he said. 'It's a Double-O. It's impossible to have a drink in the house with Varvara around. She'd be on to me about alcoholism. But we can feel free here. It's a fine brandy.'

They sat down. The brandy was very good.

'Let's have a really good drink tonight,' Sergey Sergeich continued, nibbling a lemon. 'I've always been a gay dog myself and I like having a fling now and again. That's a *must!*'

But the look in his eyes still showed that he needed something from Podgorin and was about to ask for it.

'Drink up, old man,' he went on, sighing. 'Things are really grim at the moment. Old eccentrics like me have had their day, we're finished. Idealism's not fashionable these days. It's money that rules and if you don't want to get shoved aside you must go down on your knees and worship filthy lucre. But I can't do that, it's absolutely sickening!'

'When's the auction?' asked Podgorin, to change the subject.

'August 7th. But there's no hope at all, old man, of saving Kuzminki. There's enormous arrears and the estate doesn't bring in any income, only losses every year. It's not worth the battle. Tatyana's very cut up about it, as it's her patrimony of course. But I must admit I'm rather glad. I'm no country man. My sphere is the large, noisy city, my element's the fray!'

He kept on and on, still beating about the bush and he watched Podgorin with an eagle eye, as if waiting for the right moment.

Suddenly Podgorin saw those eyes close to him and felt his breath on his face.

'My dear fellow, please save me,' Sergey Sergeich gasped. '*Please* lend me two hundred roubles!'

Podgorin wanted to say that he was hard up too and he felt that he might do better giving two hundred roubles to some poor devil or simply losing them at cards. But he was terribly embarrassed – he felt trapped in that small room with one candle and wanted to escape as soon as possible from that breathing, from those soft arms that grasped him around the waist and which already seemed to have stuck to him like glue. Hurriedly he started feeling in his pockets for his notecase where he kept money.

'Here you are,' he muttered, taking out a hundred roubles. 'I'll give you the rest later. That's all I have on me. You see, I can't refuse.' Feeling very annoyed and beginning to lose his temper he went on. 'I'm really far too soft. Only please let me have the money back later. I'm hard up too.'

'Thank you. I'm so grateful, dear chap.'

'And please stop imagining that you're an idealist.

You're as much an idealist as I'm a turkey-cock. You're simply a frivolous, indolent man, that's all.'

Sergey Sergeich sighed deeply and sat on the couch.

'My dear chap, you *are* angry,' he said. 'But if you only knew how hard things are for me! I'm going through a terrible time now. I swear it's not myself I feel sorry for, oh no! It's the wife and children. If it wasn't for my wife and children I'd have done myself in ages ago.' Suddenly his head and shoulders started shaking and he burst out sobbing.

'This really is the limit!' Podgorin said, pacing the room excitedly and feeling really furious. 'Now, what can I do with someone who has caused a great deal of harm and then starts sobbing? These tears disarm me, I'm speechless. You're sobbing, so that means you must be right.'

'Caused a great deal of harm?' Sergey Sergeich asked, rising to his feet and looking at Podgorin in amazement. 'My dear chap, what are you saying? Caused a great deal of harm? Oh, how little you know me. How little you understand me!'

'All right then, so I don't understand you, but please stop whining. It's revolting!'

'Oh, how little you know me!' Sergey Sergeich repeated, quite sincerely. 'How little!'

'Just take a look at yourself in the mirror,' Podgorin went on. 'You're no longer a young man. Soon you'll be old. It's time you stopped to think a bit and took stock of who and what you are. Spending your whole life doing nothing at all, forever indulging in empty, childish chatter, this play-acting and affectation. Doesn't it make your head go round – aren't you sick and tired of it all? Oh, it's hard going with you! You're a stupefying old bore, you are!'

With these words Podgorin left the outhouse and slammed the door. It was about the first time in his life that he had been sincere and really spoken his mind.

Shortly afterwards he was regretting having been so harsh. What was the point of talking seriously or arguing with a man who was perpetually lying, who ate and drank too much, who spent large amounts of other people's money while being quite convinced that he was an idealist and a martyr? This was a case of stupidity, or of deep-rooted bad habits that had eaten away at his organism like an illness past all cure. In any event, indignation and stern rebukes were useless in this case. Laughing at him would be more effective. One good sneer would have achieved much more than a dozen sermons!

'It's best just ignoring him,' Podgorin thought. 'Above all, not to lend him money.'

Soon afterwards he wasn't thinking about Sergey Sergeich, or about his hundred roubles. It was a calm, brooding night, very bright. Whenever Podgorin looked up at the sky on moonlit nights he had the feeling that only he and the moon were awake – everything else was either sleeping or drowsing. He gave no more thought to people or money and his mood gradually became calm and peaceful. He felt alone in this world and the sound of his own footsteps in the silence of the night seemed so mournful.

The garden was enclosed by a white stone wall. In the right-hand corner, facing the fields, stood a tower that had been built long ago, in the days of serfdom. Its lower section was of stone; the top was wooden, with a platform, a conical roof and a tall spire with a black weathercock. Down below were two gates leading straight from the garden into the fields and a staircase that creaked underfoot led up to the platform. Under the staircase some old broken armchairs had been dumped and they were bathed in the moonlight as it filtered through the gate. With their crooked upturned legs these armchairs seemed to have come to life at night and were lying in wait for someone here in the silence.

Podgorin climbed the stairs to the platform and sat down. Just beyond the fence were a boundary ditch and bank and further off were the broad fields flooded in moonlight. Podgorin knew that there was a wood exactly opposite, about two miles from the estate, and he thought that he could distinguish a dark strip in the distance. Quails and corncrakes were calling. Now and then, from the direction of the wood, came the cry of a cuckoo which couldn't sleep either.

He heard footsteps. Someone was coming across the garden towards the tower.

A dog barked.

'Beetle!' a woman's voice softly called. 'Come back, Beetle!'

He could hear someone entering the tower down below and a moment later a black dog – an old friend of Podgorin's – appeared on the bank. It stopped, looked up towards where Podgorin was sitting and wagged its tail amicably. Soon afterwards a white figure rose from the black ditch like a ghost and stopped on the bank as well. It was Nadezhda.

'Can you see something there?' she asked the dog, glancing upwards.

She didn't see Podgorin but probably sensed that he was near, since she was smiling and her pale, moonlit face was happy. The tower's black shadow stretching over the earth, far into the fields, that motionless white figure with the blissfully smiling, pale face, the black dog and both their shadows – all this was just like a dream.

'Someone *is* there,' Nadezhda said softly.

She stood waiting for him to come down or to call her up to him, so that he could at last declare his love – then both would be happy on that calm, beautiful night. White, pale, slender, very lovely in the moonlight, she awaited his caresses. She was weary of perpetually dreaming of love and happiness and was unable to conceal her feelings any longer. Her whole figure, her radiant eyes, her fixed happy smile, betrayed her innermost thoughts. But he felt awkward, shrank back and didn't make a sound, not knowing whether to speak, whether to make the habitual joke out of the situation or whether to remain silent. He felt annoyed and his only thought was that here, in a country garden on a moonlit night, close to a beautiful, loving, thoughtful girl, he felt the same apathy as on Little Bronny Street: evidently this type of romantic situation had lost its fascination, like *that* prosaic depravity. Of no consequence to him now were those meetings on moonlit nights, those white shapes with slim waists, those mysterious shadows, towers, country estates and characters such as Sergey Sergeich, and people like himself, Podgorin, with his icy indifference, his constant irritability, his inability to adapt to reality and take what it had to offer, his wearisome, obsessive craving for what did not and never could exist on earth. And now, as he sat in that tower, he would have preferred a good fireworks display, or some moonlight procession, or Varvara reciting Nekrasov's *The Railway* again. He would rather another woman was standing there on the bank where Nadezhda was: this other woman would have told him something absolutely fascinating and new that had nothing to do with love or happiness. And if she did happen to speak of love, this would have been a summons to those new, lofty, rational aspects of existence on whose threshold we are perhaps already living and of which we sometimes seem to have premonitions.

'There's no one there,' Nadezhda said.

She stood there for another minute or so, then she walked quietly towards the wood, her head bowed. The dog ran on ahead. Podgorin could see her white figure for quite a long time. 'To think how it's all turned out, though . . .' he repeated to himself as he went back to the outhouse.

He had no idea what he could say to Sergey Sergeich or Tatyana the next day or the day after that, or how he would treat Nadezhda. And he felt embarrassed, frightened and bored in advance. How was he going to fill those three long days which he had promised to spend here? He remembered the conversation about second sight and Sergey Sergeich quoting the lines:

> Before he had time to groan
> A bear came and knocked him prone.

He remembered that tomorrow, to please Tatyana, he would have to smile at those well-fed, chubby little girls – and he decided to leave.

At half past five in the morning Sergey Sergeich appeared on the terrace of the main house in his Bokhara dressing-gown and tasselled fez. Not losing a moment, Podgorin went over to him to say goodbye.

'I have to be in Moscow by ten,' he said, looking away. 'I'd completely forgotten I'm expected at the Notary Public's office. Please excuse me. When the others are up please tell them that I apologize. I'm dreadfully sorry.'

In his hurry he didn't hear Sergey Sergeich's answer and he kept looking round at the windows of the big house, afraid that the ladies might wake up and stop him going. He was ashamed he felt so nervous. He sensed that this was his last visit to Kuzminki, that he would never come back. As he drove away he glanced back several times at the outhouse where once he had spent so many happy days. But deep down he felt coldly indifferent, not at all sad.

At home the first thing he saw on the table was the note he'd received the day before: 'Dear Misha,' he read. 'You've completely forgotten us, please come and visit us soon.' And for some reason he remembered Nadezhda whirling round in the dance, her dress billowing, revealing her legs in their flesh-coloured stockings . . .

Ten minutes later he was at his desk working – and he didn't give Kuzminki another thought.

Ionych

I

When visitors to the county town of S— complained
of the monotony and boredom of life there, the local
people would reply, as if in self-defence, that the very
opposite was the case, that life there was in fact
extremely good, that the town had a library, a theatre,
a club, that there was the occasional ball and – finally
– that there were intelligent, interesting and agreeable
families with whom to make friends. And they would
single out the Turkins as the most cultivated and gifted
family.

This family lived in its own house on the main street,
next door to the Governor's. Ivan Petrovich Turkin,
a stout, handsome, dark-haired man with sideburns,
would organize amateur theatricals for charity – and
he himself played the parts of elderly generals, when
he would cough most amusingly. He had a copious
stock of funny stories, riddles and proverbs, was a great
wag and humorist, and you could never tell from his
expression whether he was serious or joking. His wife,
Vera Iosifovna, a thin, attractive woman with pince-
nez, wrote short stories and novels which she loved
reading to her guests. Their young daughter Yekaterina
Ivanovna played the piano. In short, each Turkin had

some particular talent. The Turkins were convivial hosts and cheerfully displayed their talents to their guests with great warmth and lack of pretension. Their large stone house was spacious, and cool in summer. Half of its windows opened onto a shady old garden where nightingales sang in spring. When they had visitors the clatter of knives came from the kitchen and the yard would smell of fried onion – all of which invariably heralded a lavish and tasty supper.

And no sooner had Dr Dmitry Ionych Startsev been appointed local medical officer and taken up residence at Dyalizh, about six miles away, then he too was told that – as a man of culture – he simply *must* meet the Turkins. One winter's day he was introduced to Ivan Petrovich in the street. They chatted about the weather, the theatre, cholera – and an invitation followed. One holiday in spring (it was Ascension Day), after seeing his patients, Startsev set off for town to relax a little and at the same time to do a spot of shopping. He went there on foot, without hurrying himself (as yet he had no carriage and pair), and all the way he kept humming: ''Ere I had drunk from life's cup of tears.'

In town he dined, took a stroll in the park, and then he suddenly remembered Ivan Petrovich's invitation and decided to call on the Turkins and see what kind of people they were.

'Good day – if you please!' Ivan Petrovich said, meeting him on the front steps. 'Absolutely, overwhelmingly delighted to see such a charming visitor! Come in, I'll introduce you to my good lady wife. Verochka,' he went on, introducing the doctor to his wife, 'I've been telling him that he has no right at all under Roman law to stay cooped up in that hospital – he should devote his leisure time to socializing. Isn't that so, my sweet?'

'Please sit here,' Vera Iosifovna said, seating the guest beside her. 'You are permitted to flirt with me. My husband's as jealous as Othello, but we'll try and behave so that he doesn't notice a thing.'

'Oh, my sweet little chick-chick!' Ivan Petrovich muttered tenderly, planting a kiss on her forehead. 'You've timed your visit to perfection!' he added, turning once more to his guest. 'My good lady wife's written a real whopper of a novel and she's going to read it out loud this evening.'

'Jean, my pet,' Vera Iosifovna told her husband. '*Dites que l'on nous donne du thé.*'

Startsev was introduced to Yekaterina Ivanovna, an eighteen-year-old girl who was the image of her mother – and just as thin and attractive. Her waist was slim and delicate, and her expression was still that of a child. And her youthful, already well-developed, beautiful, healthy bosom hinted at spring, true spring. Then they had tea with jam, honey, chocolates, and very tasty pastries that simply melted in one's mouth.

Towards evening more guests began to arrive and Ivan Petrovich would look at them with his laughing eyes and say: 'Good evening – if you please!'

Then they all sat in the drawing-room with very serious expressions, and Vera Iosifovna read from her novel, which began: 'The frost was getting harder . . .'

The windows were wide open and they could hear the clatter of knives in the kitchen; the smell of fried onion drifted over from the yard . . . To be sitting in those soft armchairs was highly relaxing and the lamps winked so very invitingly in the twilight of the drawing-room; and now, on an early summer's evening, when the sound of voices and laughter came from the street and the scent of lilac wafted in from outside, it was difficult to understand all that claptrap about how the frost was getting harder and 'the setting sun was illuminating with its cold rays the lonely wayfarer crossing a snowy plain'. Vera Iosifovna read how a beautiful young countess established schools, hospitals and libraries in her village and how she fell in love with a wandering artist. She read of things that never happen in real life. All the same, it was pleasantly soothing to hear about them – and they evoked such serene and delightful thoughts that one was reluctant to get up.

'Not awfully baddish!' Ivan Petrovich said softly.

One of the guests, whose thoughts were wandering far, far away as he listened, remarked: 'Yes . . . indeed . . .'

One hour passed, then another. In the municipal park close by a band was playing and a choir was singing. For five minutes after Vera Iosifovna had closed her manuscript everyone sat in silence listening to the choir singing 'By Rushlight', a song that conveyed what really happens in life and what was absent from the novel.

'Do you have your works published in magazines?' Startsev asked Vera Iosifovna.

'No,' she replied. 'I don't publish them anywhere . . .
I hide away what I've written in a cupboard. And why
publish?' she explained. 'It's not as if we need the
money.'

And for some reason everyone sighed.

'And now, Pussycat, play us something,' Ivan
Petrovich told his daughter.

They raised the piano lid and opened some music
that happened to be lying there ready. Yekaterina
Ivanovna sat down and struck the keys with both
hands. And then she immediately struck them again,
with all her might – and again and again. Her shoulders
and bosom quivered, relentlessly she kept hammering
away in the same place and it seemed that she had no
intention of stopping until she had driven those keys
deep into the piano. The drawing-room was filled with
the sound of thunder. Everything reverberated – floor,
ceiling, furniture. Yekaterina Ivanovna played a long,
difficult, monotonous passage that was interesting
solely on account of its difficulty. As Startsev listened
he visualized large boulders rolling from the top of a
high mountain, rolling and forever rolling – and he
wanted the rolling to quickly stop. And at the same
time, Yekaterina Ivanovna, her face pink from the exer-
tion, strong and brimful of energy, with a lock of
hair tumbling onto her forehead, struck him as most
attractive. And how pleasant and refreshing it was,
after a winter spent in Dyalizh among patients and
peasants, to be sitting in that drawing-room, to be
looking at that young, exquisite and most probably

innocent creature, to be listening to those deafening, tiresome, yet civilized sounds.

'Well, Pussycat! You've really excelled yourself today!' Ivan Petrovich said with tears in his eyes, rising to his feet when his daughter had finished. '"Die now Denis, you'll never write better!"'

They all surrounded and congratulated her, expressed their admiration and assured her that it was a long, long time since they had heard such a performance, while she listened in silence, faintly smiling – and triumph was written all over her figure.

'Wonderful! Excellent!' Startsev exclaimed too, yielding to the general mood of enthusiasm.

'Where did you study music?' he asked Yekaterina. 'At the Conservatoire?'

'No, I'm still only preparing for it, but in the meantime I've been having lessons with Madame Zavlovsky.'

'Did you go to the local high school?'

'Oh no!' intervened Vera Iosifovna. 'We engaged private tutors. At high school or boarding-school, you must agree, one could meet with bad influences. A growing girl should be under the influence of her mother and no one else.'

'I'm going to the Conservatoire all the same,' Yekaterina retorted.

'No, Pussycat loves her Mama. Pussycat's not going to upset Mama and Papa, is she?'

'I *will* go, I *will*!' replied Yekaterina half-joking, acting like a naughty child and stamping her little foot.

Over supper Ivan Petrovich was able to display his

talents. He told funny stories, laughing only with his eyes; he joked, he set absurd riddles and solved them himself, perpetually talking in his own weird lingo that had been cultivated by lengthy practice in the fine art of wit and which had evidently become second nature to him by now:

'A real whopper! – not awfully baddish! – thanking you most convulsively!'

But that was not all. When the guests, replete and contented, crowded in the hall, sorting out their coats and canes, Pavlushka the footman (or Peacock as he was nicknamed), a boy of about fourteen with cropped hair and chubby cheeks, kept bustling around them.

'Now, Peacock, perform!' Ivan Petrovich told him.

Peacock struck a pose and raised one arm aloft.

'Die, wretched woman!' he declaimed in tragic accents. And everyone roared with laughter.

'Most entertaining!' thought Startsev as he went out into the street. He called at a restaurant and drank some beer before setting off for Dyalizh. All the way he kept humming: 'Thy voice for me is dear and languorous.'

After a six-mile walk he went to bed, not feeling in the least tired: on the contrary, he felt that he could have walked another thirteen miles with the greatest pleasure.

'Not awfully baddish!' he remembered as he dozed off. And he burst out laughing.

II

Startsev had always been intending to visit the Turkins again, but he was so overloaded with work in the hospital that it was impossible to find a spare moment. This way more than a year passed in hard work and solitude. But one day someone from town brought him a letter in a light blue envelope.

Vera Iosifovna had long been suffering from migraine but recently, when Pussycat had been scaring her every day by threatening to go off to the Conservatoire, the attacks had become much more frequent. Every doctor in town called on the Turkins, until finally it was the district doctor's turn. Vera Iosifovna wrote him a touching letter, begging him to come and relieve her sufferings. So Startsev went and subsequently became a very frequent visitor at the Turkins' – very frequent. In point of fact, he did help Vera Iosifovna a little and she told all her friends that he was an exceptional, a truly wonderful doctor. But it was no longer the migraine that brought Startsev to the Turkins'.

He had the day off. Yekaterina Ivanovna finished her interminable, tiresome piano exercises, after which they all sat in the dining-room for a long time drinking tea, while Ivan Petrovich told one of his funny stories. But then the front door bell rang and Ivan Petrovich had to go into the hall to welcome some new visitor. Startsev took advantage of the momentary distraction and whispered to Yekaterina Ivanovna in great agitation:

'Don't torment me, for Christ's sake. I beg you! Let's go into the garden.'

She shrugged her shoulders as if at a loss to understand what he wanted from her; still, she got up and went out.

'You usually play the piano for three or four hours at a time,' he said as he followed her, 'then you sit with your mama, so I have no chance to talk to you. Please spare me a mere quarter of an hour. I beg you!'

Autumn was approaching and all was quiet and sad in the old garden; dark leaves lay thick on the paths. Already the evenings were drawing in.

'I haven't seen you the whole week,' Startsev continued. 'If you only knew what hell I've been through! Let's sit down. Please listen to what I have to say.'

Both of them had their favourite spot in the garden – the bench under the broad, old maple. And now they sat down on this bench.

'What do you want?' Yekaterina Ivanovna asked in a dry, matter-of-fact tone.

'I haven't seen you the whole week. It's been so long since I heard you speak. I passionately want to hear your voice, I *thirst* for it! Please speak.'

She captivated him by her freshness, by that naïve expression of her eyes and cheeks. Even in the way she wore her dress he saw something exceptionally charming, touching in its simplicity and innocent grace. And at the same time, despite her naïveté, she struck him as extremely intelligent and mature for her age. With someone like her he could discuss literature, art – anything he liked in fact; he could complain to her about life, about people, although during serious conversations she would sometimes suddenly start laughing quite inappropriately and run back to the house. Like almost all the young ladies of S— she read a great deal (on the whole the people of S— read very little and they said in the local library that if it weren't for girls and young Jews they might as well close the place down). This pleased Startsev immeasurably and every time they met he would excitedly ask her what she had been reading over the past few days and he would listen enchanted when she told him.

'What did you read that week we didn't meet?' he asked her now. 'Tell me, I beg you.'

'I read Pisemsky.'

'And what precisely?'

'*A Thousand Souls*,' Pussycat replied. 'And what a funny name Pisemsky had: Aleksey Feofilaktych!'

'But where are you going?' Startsev cried out in horror when she suddenly got up and went towards the house. 'I must talk to you ... there's something I must explain ... Please stay, for just five minutes! I implore you!'

She stopped as if she wanted to say something. Then she awkwardly thrust a little note into his hand and ran off into the house, where she sat down at the piano again.

'Be at the cemetery tonight at eleven o'clock by the Demetti tomb,' read Startsev.

'Well, that's really rather silly,' he thought, collecting himself. 'Why the *cemetery*? What for?'

Pussycat was obviously playing one of her little

games. Who in their right mind would want to arrange a rendezvous at night in a cemetery, miles from town, when they could easily have met in the street or the municipal park? And did it become him, a district doctor, an intelligent, respectable person, to be sighing, receiving billets-doux, hanging around cemeteries, doing things so silly that even schoolboys would laugh at them these days! What would his colleagues say if they found out?

These were Startsev's thoughts as he wandered around the tables at the club. But at half past ten he suddenly upped and went to the cemetery.

He now had his own carriage and pair – and a coachman called Panteleymon, who wore a velvet waistcoat. The moon was shining. It was quiet and warm but autumn was in the air. Near the abattoirs in one of the suburbs dogs were howling. Startsev left his carriage in a lane on the edge of town and walked the rest of the way to the cemetery. 'Everyone has his peculiar side,' he thought. 'Pussycat's rather weird too and – who knows? – perhaps she's not joking and she'll turn up.' And he surrendered to this feeble, vain hope – and it intoxicated him.

For a quarter of a mile he walked over the fields. The cemetery appeared in the distance as a dark strip – like a forest or large garden. The white stone wall, the gates came into view ... In the moonlight he could read on the gates: 'The hour is coming when ...' Startsev passed through a wicket-gate and what first caught his eye were the white crosses and tombstones on either side of a wide avenue and the black shadows cast by them and the poplars. All around, far and wide, he could see black and white, and the sleepy trees lowered their branches over the white beneath them. It seemed lighter here than in the open fields. The paw-like leaves of the maples stood out sharply against the yellow sand of the avenues and against the grave-stones, while inscriptions on monuments were clearly visible. Immediately Startsev was struck by what he was seeing for the first time in his life and what he would probably never see again: a world that was unlike any other, a world where the moonlight was so exquis-ite and soft it seemed to have its cradle here; a world where there was no life – no, not one living thing – but where, in every dark poplar, in every grave, one sensed the presence of some secret that promised peaceful, beautiful, eternal life. From those stones and faded flowers, mingling with the smell of autumnal leaves, there breathed forgiveness, sadness and peace.

All around was silence. The stars looked down from the heavens in profound humility and Startsev's foot-steps rang out so sharply, so jarringly here. Only when the chapel clock began to strike and he imagined him-self dead and buried here for ever did he have the feeling that someone was watching him and for a minute he thought that here was neither peace nor tranquillity, only the mute anguish of non-existence, of stifled despair . . .

Demetti's tomb was in the form of a shrine sur-mounted by an angel. An Italian opera company had once passed through S— and one of the female singers had died. She had been buried here and they had erected this monument. No longer was she remembered in town, but the lamp over the entrance to the shrine reflected the moonlight and seemed to be burning.

No one was there. And how could anyone think of coming here at midnight? But Startsev waited – and as if the moonlight were kindling his desires he waited passionately, imagining kisses and embraces. He sat by the monument for about half an hour, then he wandered along side-paths, hat in hand, waiting and reflecting how many women and young girls who had once been beautiful and enchanting, who had loved and burnt at night with passion, who had yielded to caresses, lay buried here. And in effect, what a terrible joke Nature plays on man – and how galling to be conscious of it!

These were Startsev's thoughts – and at the same time he wanted to shout out loud that he yearned for love, that he was waiting for love and that he must have it at all costs. Now he no longer saw slabs of white marble, but beautiful bodies; he saw figures coyly hiding in the shadows of the trees. He felt their warmth – and this yearning became all too much to bear . . .

And then, just as if a curtain had been lowered, the moon vanished behind the clouds and suddenly everything went dark. Startsev had difficulty finding the gate – all around it was dark, the darkness of an autumn night. Then he wandered around for an hour and a half, looking for the lane where he had left the carriage and pair.

'I'm so exhausted I can barely stand,' he told Panteleymon. And as he happily settled down in the carriage he thought: 'Oh, I really ought to lose some weight!'

III

Next evening he went to the Turkins' to propose to Yekaterina Ivanovna. But it happened to be an inconvenient time, since Yekaterina Ivanovna was in her room with her hairdresser having her hair done. That evening she was going to a dance at the club.

So once again he was condemned to a tea-drinking session in the dining-room. Noticing that his guest was bored and in a thoughtful mood Ivan Petrovich took some small pieces of paper from his waistcoat pocket and read out a comical letter from a German estate manager, that 'all the machinations on the estate were ruinated' and that 'all the proprieties had collapsed'.

'I bet they'll come up with a good dowry,' Startsev thought, listening absent-mindedly.

After a sleepless night he was in a state of stupor, just as if he had been given some sweetly cloying sleeping draught. His feelings were confused, but warm and joyful – and at the same time a cold, obdurate, small section of his brain kept reasoning: 'Stop before it's too late! Is she the right kind of wife for you? She's spoilt, capricious, she sleeps until two in the afternoon. But you're a sacristan's son, a country doctor . . .'

'Well, what of it?' he thought. 'It doesn't matter.'

'What's more, if you marry her,' continued the small

voice, 'her family will make you give up your country practice and you'll have to move to town.'

'What of it?' he thought. 'Nothing wrong with living in town. And there'll be a dowry, we'll set up house together . . .'

At last in came Yekaterina Ivanovna, wearing a ball gown, décolletée, looking very pretty and elegant. Startsev couldn't admire her enough and such was his delight that he was at a loss for words and could only look on and smile.

She began to make her farewells and he stood up – there was nothing more for him to stay for – saying that it was time he went home as his patients were waiting.

'Well, it can't be helped, you'd better go,' said Ivan Petrovich. 'At the same time you could give Pussycat a lift to the club.'

Outside it was drizzling and very dark, and only from Panteleymon's hoarse cough could they tell where the carriage was. They put the hood up.

'Such a fright will set you alight,' Ivan Petrovich said, seating his daughter in the carriage. 'If you lie – it's as nice as pie . . . ! Off you go now. Goodbye – if you please!'

They drove off.

'Last night I went to the cemetery,' Startsev began. 'How unkind, how heartless of you!'

'You went to the cemetery?'

'Yes, I went and waited for you until two o'clock. It was sheer hell.'

Delighted to have played such a cunning trick on

the man who loved her, and that she was the object of such fervent passion, Yekaterina Ivanovna burst out laughing – and then she suddenly screamed with terror, for just then the horses turned sharply through the club gates, making the carriage lurch violently. Startsev put his arms around Yekaterina Ivanovna's waist as she clung to him in her fright.

He could not control himself and kissed her lips and chin passionately, holding her in an even tighter embrace.

'That will do!' she said curtly.

A moment later she was gone from the carriage and the policeman standing at the lighted entrance to the club shouted at Panteleymon in a very ugly voice:

'What yer stopped there for, you oaf! Move on!'

Startsev went home but he soon returned. Wearing borrowed coat and tails and a stiff white cravat which somehow kept sticking up as if wanting to slide off his collar, he sat at midnight in the club lounge and told Yekaterina Ivanovna in passionate terms:

'Oh, those who have never loved – how little do they know! I think that no one has ever truly described love – and how could anyone describe that tender, joyful, agonizing feeling! Anyone who has but once experienced it would never even think of putting it into words! But what's the point of preambles and descriptions? Why this superfluous eloquence? My love has no bounds. I'm asking you, begging you,' Startsev at last managed to say, 'to be my wife!'

'Dmitry Ionych,' Yekaterina Ivanovna said with a very serious expression after pausing for thought,

'Dmitry Ionych, I'm most grateful for the honour and I respect you, but . . .' She stood up and continued standing. 'I'm sorry, I cannot be your wife. Let's talk seriously. As you know, Dmitry Ionych, I love art more than anything in the world. I'm mad about music, I simply adore it. I've dedicated my whole life to it. I want to be a concert pianist. I want fame, success, freedom. But you want me to go on living in this town, to carry on with this empty, useless life that's become quite unbearable for me. To be your *wife* . . . oh no, I'm sorry! One must always aspire towards some lofty, brilliant goal, but family life would tie me down for ever. Dmitry Ionych' (at this she produced a barely perceptible smile since, when saying Dmitry Ionych the name Aleksey Feofilaktych came to mind), 'Dmitry Ionych, you're a kind, honourable, clever man, you're the best of all . . .' (here her eyes filled with tears), 'I feel for you with all my heart, but . . . but you must understand . . .'

And to avoid bursting into tears she turned away and walked out of the lounge.

Startsev's heart stopped pounding. As he went out of the club into the street the first thing he did was tear off that stiff cravat and heave a deep sigh of relief. He felt rather ashamed and his pride was hurt – he had not expected a refusal. And he just could not believe that all his dreams, yearnings and hopes had led to such a stupid conclusion, as if it were all a trivial little play performed by amateurs. And he regretted having felt as he did, he regretted having loved – so much so that he came close to sobbing out loud or

played cards or enjoyed a meal with any resident of that town, then that person would be inoffensive, good-natured and even quite intelligent. But the moment one started a conversation about something that was inedible, such as politics or science, then the other person would either be stumped or give vent to such absurd and vicious ideas that one could only give it up as a bad job and make one's exit. Whenever Startsev tried to start a conversation, even with a citizen of liberal views – for example, concerning the immense progress that humanity was making, thank God, and that, given time, it would be able to dispense with passports or the death penalty – he would be greeted with distrustful, sidelong glances and asked: 'In that case, anyone could cut the throat of anyone he wanted to in the street, couldn't he?' And whenever he had supper or tea in company and ventured to say that one had to work hard, that life was impossible without hard work, everyone took it as a personal insult, got angry and launched into the most tiresome disputations. Yet these townspeople did nothing, absolutely nothing, and they were interested in nothing. So Startsev avoided conversations (it was impossible to think of anything to discuss with them), confining himself to eating and playing whist with them. Whenever he happened to be in a house where there was some family celebration and he was invited to stay for supper, he would sit down and eat in silence, staring blankly at his plate. And everything they happened to be discussing struck him as uninteresting, unfair, stupid; but despite his irritation and exasperation he remained silent. These stony silences and his habit of staring at his plate earned him the name 'Snooty Pole' in that town, although he had never been Polish.

He shunned diversions such as the theatre and concerts, but took great pleasure in playing whist every evening, until two o'clock in the morning. But there was one other diversion to which he became gradually, imperceptibly drawn. This was in the evenings, when he took from his pockets the banknotes he had earned from his practice – and his pockets often happened to be stuffed with seventy roubles' worth of yellow or green notes that reeked of perfume, vinegar, incense and train oil. When he had amassed a few hundred he would take them to the Mutual Credit Bank and pay them into his current account.

During the entire four years after Yekaterina Ivanovna's departure for Moscow he visited the Turkins only twice, at the invitation of Vera Iosifovna, whom he was still treating for migraine. Every summer Yekaterina Ivanovna would come to stay with her parents but as things turned out he did not see her even once.

But four years had now passed. One calm, warm morning he was brought a letter at the hospital, in which Vera Iosifovna wrote that she missed him very much and begged him to come and see her without fail and relieve her sufferings – that day happened to be her birthday. There was a PS: 'I join in Mama's request. K.'

Startsev thought for a while and that evening he drove over to the Turkins'.

'Ah, good evening – if you please!' Ivan Petrovich greeted him. Only his eyes were smiling. *'Bonjourez-vous!'*

Vera Iosifovna had aged considerably and her hair was white now. She shook Startsev's hand, and sighed affectedly.

'Doctor!' she exclaimed. 'You don't want to flirt with me, you never call on us, so I must be too old for you. But my young daughter's arrived, perhaps she'll have more luck!'

And Pussycat? She had grown thinner, paler, prettier and shapelier. But now she was a fully-fledged Yekaterina Ivanovna and not a Pussycat. Gone were that freshness and expression of childlike innocence. And in her look and manners there was something new, a hesitancy and air of guilt, as if here, in the Turkins' house, she no longer felt at home.

'It's been simply ages!' she said, offering Startsev her hand – and her heart was visibly pounding. Peering into his face intently, quizzically, she continued: 'How you've put on weight! You've acquired a tan, you've matured, but on the whole you haven't changed very much.'

And even now he liked her – very much so. But something was lacking, or there was something superfluous – he himself couldn't put his finger on it, but it prevented him from feeling as he did before. He did not like her pallor, her new expression, that weak smile, her voice. And a little later he didn't like her dress, or the armchair she was sitting in; something about the past, when he had nearly married her, displeased him. He recalled his love, those dreams and hopes that had disturbed him four years before, and he felt uncomfortable.

They had tea and cakes. Then Vera Iosifovna read her novel out loud – about things that never happen in real life – and Startsev listened, looked at her grey handsome head and waited for her to finish.

'A mediocrity is not someone who's no good at writing stories,' he thought. 'It's someone who writes them but can't keep quiet about it.'

'Not awfully baddish!' Ivan Petrovich commented.

Then Yekaterina Ivanovna played the piano long and noisily, and when she had finished there followed lengthy expressions of gratitude and admiration.

'Lucky I didn't marry her,' thought Startsev.

She glanced at him and was evidently waiting for him to suggest going out into the garden, but he said nothing.

'Let's have a little talk,' she said, going over to him. 'How are you getting on? What's your news? How are things? All this time I've been thinking of you,' she continued nervously. 'I wanted to write to you, to come and see you in Dyalizh myself. In fact I actually decided to come but I changed my mind. Heaven knows what you think of me now. I've been so excited waiting for you today. For heaven's sake, let's go into the garden.'

They went into the garden and sat down on the bench under the old maple, as they had done four years before. It was dark.

'Well, how are things?' Yekaterina Ivanovna asked.

'All right, I get by,' Startsev replied.

And he could think of nothing more to say. They both fell silent.

'I'm so excited,' Yekaterina Ivanovna said, covering her face with her hands, 'but don't take any notice. I *so* enjoy being at home. I'm so glad to see everyone and it takes getting used to. So many memories! I thought we'd be talking non-stop, until the early hours.'

And now he saw her face close up, her sparkling eyes; and here, in the darkness, she looked younger than in the room and even her former childlike expression seemed to have returned. And in fact she gazed at him with naïve curiosity, as if she wanted to have a closer look, to understand the man who had once loved her so passionately, so tenderly, so unhappily. Her eyes thanked him for that love. And he recalled everything that had happened, down to the very last detail – how he had wandered around the cemetery, how he had gone home exhausted towards morning; and suddenly he felt sad and he regretted the past. A tiny flame flickered in his heart.

'Do you remember when I gave you a lift that evening to the club?' he asked. 'It was raining then, and dark . . .'

The flame was still flickering in his heart and he felt the urge to speak, to complain about life . . .

'Oh!' he sighed. 'You ask me how things are, what kind of lives we lead here? Well, we don't lead any kind of life. We grow old, get fat, go to seed. Day after day life drags on in its lacklustre way, no impressions, no thoughts . . . During the day I make money, in the evening there's the club and the company of cardsharpers, alcoholics and loudmouths whom I cannot stand. So what's good about it?'

'But there's your work, a noble purpose in life. You used to love talking about your hospital. I was rather strange then, I imagined myself as a great pianist. Now all young women play the piano and I played like everyone else and there was nothing special about me. I'm as much a concert pianist as Mama's a writer. Of course, I didn't understand you then, but afterwards, in Moscow, I often thought of you. In fact, I thought of nothing else. What bliss to be a country doctor, to help the suffering, to serve the common people! What utter bliss!' Yekaterina repeated rapturously. 'Whenever I thought of you in Moscow you struck me as idealistic, lofty . . .'

He stood up to go back to his house. She took hold of his arm.

'You are the best person I've ever known in my life,' she went on. 'We'll see each other, we'll talk, won't we? *Promise* me. I'm no concert pianist, I've no illusions about myself and when you're with me I shall neither play nor talk about music.'

Three days later Peacock brought him a letter from Yekaterina Ivanovna.

'You never come and see us. Why?' she wrote. 'I'm afraid that you don't feel the same towards us any more. I'm afraid – and this thought alone terrifies me. Please set my mind at rest, *please* come and tell me that everything's all right. I *must* talk to you. Your Y.T.'

After reading this letter he pondered for a moment and then he told Peacock:

'Tell them, dear chap, that I can't come today, I'm too busy. Tell them I'll come and see them in about three days.'

But three days passed, a week passed and still he didn't go. Once, when he was driving past the Turkins' house, he remembered that he really should call on them, if only for a few minutes, but on reflection he decided against it.

And he never visited the Turkins again.

V

Several years have passed. Startsev has put on even more weight, grown flabby, has difficulty breathing and walks with his head thrown back. When he drives along in his carriage with three-horse team and bells, puffy and red-faced, and Panteleymon, likewise puffy and red-faced, with fleshy neck, sits on the box with his straight, seemingly wooden arms thrust forward, shouting at passers-by 'Keep to the right!', the effect is truly awe-inspiring and it seems that here comes a pagan god and no ordinary mortal. He has an enormous practice in town, he has no time for relaxation, and now he owns an estate, and two houses in town: he's looking for a third house that would bring in more income and whenever they talk of some house up for auction at the Mutual Credit Bank, then, without standing on ceremony, he marches right into the house, goes through all the rooms, ignoring half-naked women and children, who look at him in fear and trembling, pokes every door with his stick and says:

'Is this the study? Is this the bedroom? And what's *this*?'

And he breathes heavily and wipes the sweat from his brow.

He has much to preoccupy him, but he still doesn't give up his place on the local council. Greed has triumphed and he always wants to be everywhere at the right time. He's called simply Ionych in Dyalizh and in town. 'Where's old Ionych going?' or 'Shall we invite Ionych to a committee meeting?' they say.

Probably because his throat is bloated his voice has changed and become reedy and harsh. His personality has changed too: he's heavy-going now, irritable. When he sees patients he normally gets angry and impatiently bangs his stick on the floor.

'Please reply to the question! Don't argue!' he shouts in his jarring voice. In fact, he's a real lone wolf. Life is a bore, nothing interests him.

The whole time he lived in Dyalizh his love for Pussycat was his only joy and probably his last. He plays whist every evening at the club and then he sits on his own at the big table and has supper. He's waited upon by Ivan, the oldest and most venerable club servant. He's served the Lafite No. 17 and every single person there – the senior members and the footmen – knows his likes and dislikes and does his utmost to please him, otherwise he might suddenly lose his temper and start banging his stick on the floor.

When he has supper he turns round from time to

time and joins in some conversation: 'Who are you talking about? Eh? *Who?*'

And when someone at a neighbouring table happens to start discussing the Turkins he asks: 'Which Turkins do you mean? The ones whose daughter plays the piano?'

And that's all one can say about him.

And the Turkins? Ivan Petrovich hasn't aged, hasn't changed one bit and he's joking and telling his funny stories as always. And Vera Iosifovna reads her novels to her guests as eagerly as ever, with warmth and unpretentiousness. Pussycat plays the piano every day, for hours at a time. She has aged noticeably, suffers from ill health and every autumn she goes to the Crimea with her mother. When he sees them off at the station, Ivan Petrovich wipes the tears from his eyes as the train pulls out.

'Goodbye – if you please!' he shouts.

And he waves his handkerchief.

The Lady with the Little Dog

I

People said that there was a new arrival on the Promenade: a lady with a little dog. Dmitry Dmitrich Gurov, who had already spent a fortnight in Yalta and who was by now used to the life there, had also begun to take an interest in new arrivals. As he sat on the terrace of Vernet's restaurant he saw a young, fair-haired woman walking along the Promenade, not very tall and wearing a beret. A white Pomeranian trotted after her.

And then he came across her several times a day in the municipal park and the square. She was always alone, always wearing that beret, always with the white Pomeranian. No one knew who she was and people simply called her 'The lady with the little dog'.

'If she's here without husband or friends,' Gurov reasoned, 'then it wouldn't be a bad idea if I got to know her.'

He was not yet forty, but already he had a twelve-year-old daughter and two schoolboy sons. He had been married off while still quite young, as a second-year student, and now his wife seemed about half as old again as he was. She was a tall, black-browed woman, plain-spoken, pretentious, respectable and – as she was fond of claiming – 'a thinking woman'.

She was an avid reader, followed the latest reforms in spelling, called her husband Demetrius instead of Dmitry. But in secret he considered her not very bright, narrow-minded and unrefined. He was afraid of her and disliked being at home. He had begun deceiving her a long time ago, had frequently been unfaithful – which was probably why he always spoke disparagingly of women and whenever they were discussed in his company he would call them an 'inferior breed'.

He felt that he had learnt sufficiently from bitter experience to call them by whatever name he liked, yet, for all that, he could not have survived two days without his 'inferior breed'. He was bored in male company, not very talkative and offhand. But with women he felt free, knowing what to talk to them about and how to behave. Even saying nothing at all to them was easy for him. There was something attractive, elusive in his appearance, in his character – in his whole personality – that appealed to women and lured them to him. He was well aware of this and some power similarly attracted him.

Repeated – and in fact bitter – experience had long taught him that every affair, which at first adds spice and variety to life and seems such a charming, light-hearted adventure, inevitably develops into an enormous, extra-ordinarily complex problem with respectable people – especially Muscovites, who are so hesitant, so inhibited – until finally the whole situation becomes a real night-mare. But on every new encounter with an interesting woman all this experience was somehow forgotten and he simply wanted to enjoy life – and it all seemed so easy and amusing.

So, late one afternoon, he was dining at an open-air restaurant when the lady in the beret wandered over and sat at the table next to him. Her expression, the way she walked, her clothes, her hairstyle – all this told him that she was a socially respectable, married woman, that she was in Yalta for the first time, alone and bored.

There was a great deal of untruth in all those stories about the laxity of morals in that town and he despised them, knowing that such fictions are invented by people who would willingly have erred – if they'd had the chance. But when the lady seated herself about three paces away from him at the next table, those stories of easy conquests, of trips to the mountains came to mind; and the alluring thought of a swift, fleeting affair, of a romance with a strange woman whose name he didn't even know, suddenly possessed him.

Gently, he coaxed the dog over and when it came up to him he wagged his finger. The dog growled. Gurov wagged his finger again.

The lady glanced at him and immediately lowered her eyes.

'He doesn't bite,' she said, blushing.

'May I give him a bone?' he asked. And when she nodded he said affably:

'Have you been long in Yalta, madam?'

'About five days.'

'I've almost survived my second week here.'

There was a brief pause.

'The time passes quickly, but it's still so boring here!' she said, without looking at him.

'That's the done thing – to say it's boring there! Your average tripper who lives very nicely if you please in some backwater like Belyov or Zhizdra never gets bored there, but the moment he comes here he says: "Oh, what a bore! Oh, all this dust!" You'd think he'd just breezed in from sunny Granada!'

She laughed. They both carried on eating in silence, like strangers. But after dinner they wandered off together and then there began that inconsequential, light-hearted conversation of people who have no ties, who are contented, who could not care less where they go or what they talk about. As they walked they talked about the unusual light on the sea. The water was the soft, warm colour of lilac and a golden strip of moonlight lay across it. They talked about how humid it was after the heat of the day. Gurov told her he was a Muscovite, a graduate in literature but working in a bank. At one time he had trained as an opera singer but had given it up; and he owned two houses in Moscow. From her he learnt that she had grown up in St Petersburg but had got married in S—, where she had been living for the past two years; that she intended staying another month in Yalta, after which her husband – who also needed a break – might possibly come and fetch her. She was quite unable to explain where her husband worked – whether he was with the rural or county council – and this she herself found very funny. And Gurov discovered that her name was Anna Sergeyevna.

Later, back in his hotel room, he thought about her. He was bound to meet her tomorrow, of that there was no doubt. As he went to bed he remembered that she had only recently left boarding-school, that she had been a schoolgirl just like his own daughter – and he remembered how much hesitancy, how much awkwardness there was in her laughter, in the way she talked to a stranger – it must have been the very first time in her life that she had been on her own, in such surroundings, where men followed her, eyed her and spoke to her with one secret aim in mind, which she could hardly fail to guess. He recalled her slender, frail neck, her beautiful grey eyes.

'Still, there's something pathetic about her,' he thought as he fell asleep.

II

A week had passed since their first encounter. It was a holiday. Indoors it was stifling and the wind swept the dust in swirling clouds down the streets, tearing off people's hats. All day one felt thirsty and Gurov kept going to the restaurant to fetch Anna Sergeyevna cordials or ice-cream. But there was no escaping the heat.

In the evening, when the wind had dropped, they went down to the pier to watch a steamer arrive. Crowds of people were strolling on the landing-stage: they were all there to meet someone and held bunches of flowers. Two distinguishing features of the Yalta smart set caught one's attention: the older women dressed like young girls and there were lots of generals.

The steamer arrived late – after sunset – owing to rough seas, and she swung about for some time before putting in at the jetty. Anna Sergeyevna peered at the boat and passengers through her lorgnette, as if trying to make out some people she knew, and when she turned to Gurov her eyes were sparkling. She talked a lot; her questions were abrupt and she immediately forgot what she had asked. Then she lost her lorgnette in the crowd.

The smartly dressed crowd dispersed, no more faces were to be seen; the wind had dropped completely and Gurov and Anna Sergeyevna still stood there, as if waiting for someone else to disembark. Anna Sergeyevna was silent now, sniffing her flowers and not looking at Gurov.

'The weather's improved a bit, now it's evening,' he said. 'So, where shall we go? How about driving out somewhere?'

She made no reply.

Then he stared at her – and he suddenly embraced her and kissed her lips. He was steeped in the fragrance, the dampness of the flowers and at once he looked around in fright: had anyone seen them?

'Let's go to your place,' he said softly.

And together they walked away, quickly.

Her room was stuffy and smelt of the perfume she had bought in the Japanese shop. Looking at her now Gurov thought: 'The encounters one has in life!' He still remembered those carefree, light-hearted women in his past, so happy in their love and grateful to him for their happiness – however short-lived. And he recalled women who, like his wife, made love insincerely, with too much talk, affectedly, hysterically, with an expression that seemed to say that it was neither love nor passion, but something more significant. And he recalled two or three very beautiful, cold women across whose faces there suddenly flashed a predatory expression, a stubborn desire to seize, to snatch from life more than it could provide . . . and these women were no longer young; they were capricious, irrational, domineering and unintelligent. And when Gurov cooled towards them their beauty aroused hatred in him and the lace on their underclothes seemed like fish scales.

But here there was that same hesitancy, that same discomfiture, that gaucheness of inexperienced youth. And there was an air of embarrassment, as if someone had just knocked at the door. In her own particular, very serious way, Anna Sergeyevna, that lady with the little dog, regarded what had happened just as if it were her downfall. So it seemed – and it was all very weird and out of place. Her features sank and faded, and her long hair hung sadly on each side of her face. She struck a pensive, dejected pose, like the woman taken in adultery in an old-fashioned painting.

'This is wrong,' she said. 'You'll be the first to lose respect for me now.'

On the table was a water-melon. Gurov cut himself a slice and slowly started eating it. Half an hour, at least, passed in silence.

Anna Sergeyevna looked most touching. She had that air of genuine, pure innocence of a woman with little experience of life. The solitary candle burning on the table barely illuminated her face, but he could see that she was obviously suffering.

'Why should I lose my respect for you?' Gurov asked. 'You don't know what you're saying.'

'May God forgive me!' she said – and her eyes filled with tears. 'It's terrible.'

'You seem to be defending yourself.'

'How can I defend myself? I'm a wicked, vile woman. I despise myself and I'm not going to make any excuses. It's not my husband but myself I've deceived. And I don't mean only just now, but for a long time. My husband's a fine honest man, but he's no more than a lackey. What does he do in that office of his? I've no idea. But I do know he's a mere lackey. I was twenty when I married him and dying from curiosity; but I wanted something better. Surely there must be a different kind of life, I told myself. I wanted to live life to the full, to enjoy life . . . to enjoy it! I was burning with curiosity. You won't understand this, but I swear that my feelings ran away with me, something was happening to me and there was no holding me back. So I told my husband I was ill and I came here . . . And ever since I've been going around as if intoxicated, like someone demented. So, now I'm a vulgar, worthless woman whom everyone has the right to despise.'

Gurov found all this very boring. He was irritated by her naïve tone, by that sudden, untimely remorse.

But for the tears in her eyes he would have thought she was joking or play-acting.

'I don't understand,' he said softly. 'What is it you want?'

She buried her face on his chest and clung to him.

'Please, please believe me, I beg you,' she said. 'I yearn for a pure, honest life. Sin revolts me. I myself don't know what I'm doing. Simple folk say: "The devil's led me astray" – and I can honestly say that the devil's led *me* astray.'

'That's enough, enough,' he muttered.

He gazed into her staring, frightened eyes, kissed her and spoke softly and gently, so that gradually she grew calmer and her gaiety returned. They both started laughing.

Later, after they had gone out, there wasn't a soul to be seen on the Promenade and that town with its cypresses seemed completely dead; but the sea still roared as it broke on the shore. A small launch with its little lamp sleepily glimmering was tossing on the waves.

They took a cab and drove to Oreanda.

'I've just discovered your name downstairs in the lobby. The board says "von Diederitz",' Gurov said. 'Is your husband German?'

'No. I think his grandfather was, but he's Russian.'

In Oreanda they sat on a bench near the church and looked down at the sea without saying a word. Yalta was barely visible through the morning mist; white clouds lay motionless on the mountain tops. Not one leaf stirred on the trees, cicadas chirped, and the monotonous, hollow roar of the sea that reached them from below spoke of peace, of that eternal slumber that awaits us. And so it roared down below when neither Yalta nor Oreanda existed. It was roaring now and would continue its hollow, indifferent booming when we are no more. And in this permanency, in this utter indifference to the life and death of every one of us there perhaps lies hidden a pledge of our eternal salvation, of never-ceasing progress of life upon earth, of the never-ceasing march towards perfection. As he sat there beside that young woman who seemed so beautiful at daybreak, soothed and enchanted at the sight of those magical surroundings – sea, mountains, clouds, wide skies – Gurov reflected that, if one thought hard about it, everything on earth was truly beautiful except those things we ourselves think of and do when we forget the higher aims of existence and our human dignity.

Someone came up – probably a watchman – glanced at them and went away. And even in this little incident there seemed to be something mysterious – and beautiful too. They could see the steamer arriving from Feodosiya, illuminated by the sunrise, its lights extinguished.

'There's dew on the grass,' Anna Sergeyevna said after a pause.

'Yes, it's time to go back.'

They returned to town.

After this they met on the Promenade at noon every day, had lunch together, dinner together, strolled and admired the sea. She complained that she was sleeping badly, that she had palpitations and she asked him those same questions again, moved by jealousy, or fear that he did not respect her enough. And when they were in the square or municipal gardens, when no one was near, he would suddenly draw her to him and kiss her passionately. This complete idleness, the kisses in broad daylight when they would look around, afraid that someone had seen them, the heat, the smell of the sea and constant glimpses of those smartly dressed, well-fed people, seemed to transform him. He told Anna Sergeyevna how lovely she was, how seductive; he was impatient in his passion and did not leave her side for one moment. But she often became pensive and constantly asked him to admit that he had no respect for her, that he didn't love her at all and could only see her as a vulgar woman. Almost every day, in the late evening, they would drive out somewhere, to Oreanda or the waterfall. The walks they took were a great success and every time they went their impressions were invariably beautiful and majestic.

Her husband was expected to arrive soon, but a letter came in which he told her that he had eye trouble and begged his wife to return as soon as possible. Anna Sergeyevna hurried.

'It's a good thing I'm leaving,' Anna Sergeyevna said. 'It's fate.'

She went by carriage and he rode with her. The drive took nearly a whole day. When she took her seat in the express train she said after the second departure bell:

'Let me look at you again ... one last look. There ...'

She was not crying, but she looked sad, as if she were ill, and her face was trembling.

'I shall think of you ... I shall remember you ...' she said. 'God bless you – and take care of yourself. Don't think badly of me. This is our final farewell – it must be, since we never should have met ... Well, God bless you.'

The train swiftly drew out of the station, its lights soon vanished and a minute later its noise had died away, as though everything had deliberately conspired to put a speedy end to that sweet abandon, to that madness. Alone on the platform, gazing into the murky distance, Gurov listened to the chirring of the grass-hoppers and the humming of the telegraph wires, and he felt that he had just woken up. So, this was just another adventure or event in his life, he reflected, and that too was over now, leaving only the memory ... He was deeply moved and sad, and he felt a slight twinge of regret: that young woman, whom he would never see again, had not been happy with him, had she? He had been kind and affectionate, yet in his attitude, his tone and caresses, there had been a hint of casual mockery, of the rather coarse arrogance of a victorious male who, besides anything else, was twice her age. The whole time she had called him kind, exceptional, high-minded: obviously she had not seen him in his true colours, therefore he must have been unintentionally deceiving her ...

Here at the station there was already a breath of autumn in the air and the evening was cool.

'It's time I went north too', Gurov thought, leaving the platform. 'It's time!'

III

Back home in Moscow it was already like winter; the stoves had been lit; it was dark in the mornings when the children were getting ready for school and having their breakfast, so Nanny would briefly light the lamp. The frosts had set in. When the first snow falls, on the first day of sleigh-rides, it is so delightful to see the white ground and the white roofs. The air is so soft and so marvellous to breathe – and at such times one remembers the days of one's youth. The old limes and birches, white with hoarfrost, have a welcoming look – they are closer to one's heart than cypresses or palms and beside them one has no desire to think of mountains and sea.

Gurov was a Muscovite and he returned to Moscow on a fine, frosty day. When he put on his fur coat and warm gloves, and strolled down the Petrovka, when he heard the sound of bells on Saturday evening, that recent trip and the places he had visited lost all their enchantment. Gradually he immersed himself in Moscow life, hungrily reading three newspapers a day whilst claiming that he didn't read any Moscow papers, on principle. Once again he could not resist the temptation of restaurants, clubs, dinner parties, anniversary celebrations; he was flattered that famous lawyers and artists visited him and that he played cards with a professor at the Doctors' Club. He could polish off a whole portion of Moscow hotpot straight from the pan.

After another month or two the memory of Anna Sergeyevna would become misted over, so it seemed, and only occasionally would he dream of her touching smile – just as he dreamt of others. But more than a month went by, deep winter set in, and he remembered Anna Sergeyevna as vividly as if he had parted from her yesterday. And those memories became even more vivid. Whether he heard in his study, in the quiet of evening, the voices of his children preparing their lessons, or a sentimental song, or an organ in a restaurant, whether the blizzard howled in the stove, everything would suddenly spring to life in his memory: the events on the jetty, that early, misty morning in the mountains, that steamer from Feodosiya and those kisses. For a long time he paced his room, reminiscing and smiling – and then those memories turned into dreams and the past merged in his imagination with what would be. He did not simply dream of Anna Sergeyevna – she followed him everywhere, like a shadow, watching him. When he closed his eyes he saw her as though she were there before him and she seemed prettier, younger, gentler than before. And he considered himself a better person than he had been in Yalta. In the evenings she would look at him from the bookcase, from the fireplace, from a corner; he could hear her breathing, the gentle rustle of her dress.

In the street he followed women with his eyes, seeking someone who resembled her.

And now he was tormented by a strong desire to share his memories with someone. But it was impossible to talk about his love with anyone in the house – and there was no one outside it. Certainly not with his tenants or colleagues at the bank! And what was there to discuss? Had he really been in love? Had there been something beautiful, romantic, edifying or even interesting in his relations with Anna Sergeyevna? And so he was forced to talk about love and women in the vaguest terms and no one could guess what he was trying to say. Only his wife raised her dark eyebrows and said:

'Really, Demetrius! The role of ladies' man doesn't suit you one bit . . .'

One night, as he left the Doctors' Club with his partner – a civil servant – he was unable to hold back any more and said:

'If you only knew what an enchanting woman I met in Yalta!'

The civil servant climbed into his sledge and drove off. But then he suddenly turned round and called out:

'Dmitry Dmitrich!'

'What?'

'You were right the other day – the sturgeon *was* off!'

This trite remark for some reason suddenly nettled Gurov, striking him as degrading and dirty. What barbarous manners, what faces! What meaningless nights, what dismal, unmemorable days! Frenetic card games, gluttony, constant conversations about the same old thing. Those pointless business affairs and perpetual conversations – always on the same theme – were commandeering the best part of his time, his best strength, so that in the end there remained only a limited, humdrum life, just trivial nonsense. And it was impossible to run away, to escape – one might as well be in a lunatic asylum or a convict squad!

Gurov was so exasperated he did not sleep the whole night, and he suffered from a headache the whole day long. And on following nights too he slept badly, sitting up in his bed the whole time thinking, or pacing his room from corner to corner. The children bored him, he didn't want to go anywhere or talk about anything.

During the Christmas holidays he packed his things and told his wife that he was going to St Petersburg on behalf of a certain young man he wanted to help – and he went to S—. Why? He himself was not sure. But he wanted to see Anna Sergeyevna again, to arrange a meeting – if that were possible.

He arrived at S— in the morning and took the best room in the hotel, where the entire floor was fitted from wall to wall with a carpet the colour of grey army cloth; on the table was an inkstand, grey with dust, in the form of a mounted horseman holding his hat in his uplifted hand and whose head had been broken off.

The porter told him all he needed to know: von Dodderfits (this was how he pronounced von Diederitz) was living on Old Pottery Street, in his own house, not far from the hospital. He lived lavishly, on the grand scale, kept his own horses and was known by everyone in town.

Without hurrying Gurov strolled down Old Pottery Street and found the house. Immediately opposite stretched a long grey fence topped with nails.

'That fence is enough to make you want to run away', Gurov thought, looking now at the windows, now at the fence.

It was a holiday, he reflected, and local government offices would be closed – therefore her husband was probably at home . . . In any event, it would have been tactless to go into the house and embarrass her. But if he were to send a note it would most likely fall into the husband's hands and this would ruin everything. Best of all was to trust to luck. So he continued walking along the street, by the fence, waiting for his opportunity. He watched how a beggar went through the gates and was set upon by dogs; and then, an hour later, he heard the faint, indistinct sounds of a piano. Anna Sergeyevna must be playing. Suddenly the front door opened and out came some old lady followed by that familiar white Pomeranian. Gurov wanted to call the dog, but his heart suddenly started pounding and he was too excited to remember the dog's name.

He carried on walking, hating that grey fence more and more. By now he was so irritated that he was convinced Anna Sergeyevna had forgotten him and was perhaps already dallying with someone else – which was only natural with a young woman forced to look at that damned fence from morning to night. He returned to his hotel room and sat on the sofa for a long time, not knowing what to do. Then he had dinner, after which he had a long sleep.

'How stupid and upsetting it all is!' he thought as he awoke and peered at the dark windows; it was already evening. 'Well, now that I've had a good sleep what shall I do tonight?'

He sat on the bed that was covered with a cheap, grey hospital-like blanket and in his irritation he mocked himself: 'So much for ladies with little dogs! So much for holiday adventures . . . Now I'm stuck in this hole!'

At the railway station that morning his attention had been caught by a poster that advertised in bold lettering the first night of *The Geisha*. He remembered this now and drove to the theatre.

'It's very likely she goes to first nights', he thought.

The theatre was full and, as in all local theatres, there was a thick haze above the chandeliers; the gallery was noisy and excited. In the first row, before the performance began, the local dandies were standing with their arms crossed behind their backs. And in front, in the Governor's box, sat the Governor's daughter sporting a feather boa, while the Governor himself humbly hid behind the *portière*, so that only his hands were visible. The curtain shook, the orchestra took an age to tune up. All this time the audience were entering and taking their seats. Gurov looked eagerly around him.

And in came Anna Sergeyevna. She sat in the third row and when Gurov looked at her his heart seemed to miss a beat: now it was plain to him that no one in the whole world was closer, dearer and more important to him than she was. That little woman, not remarkable in any way, lost in that provincial crowd, with a vulgar lorgnette in her hand, now filled his whole life, was his sorrow, his joy, the only happiness that he now wished for himself. And to the sounds of that atrocious orchestra, of those wretched fiddlers, he thought how lovely she was. He thought – and he dreamed.

A young man with short side-whiskers, very tall and stooping, entered with Anna Sergeyevna and sat next to her. With every step he shook his head and he seemed to be perpetually bowing. Probably he was the husband whom she had called 'lackey' in Yalta in a fit of pique. And indeed, in his lanky figure, in his side-whiskers, in that slight baldness, there was something of a flunkey's subservience. He had a sickly smile and in his buttonhole there gleamed the badge of some learned society – just like the number on a flunkey's jacket.

In the first interval the husband went out for a smoke, while she remained in her seat. Gurov, who was also in the stalls, went up to her and forced a smile as he said in a trembling voice:

'Good evening!'

She looked at him and turned pale. Then she looked again, was horrified and could not believe her eyes, tightly clasping her fan and lorgnette and obviously trying hard to stop herself fainting. Neither said a word. She sat there, he stood, alarmed at her embarrassment and not daring to sit next to her. The fiddles and flutes began to tune up and suddenly they felt terrified – it seemed they were being scrutinized from every box. But then she stood up and quickly went towards the exit. He followed her and they both walked aimlessly along the corridors, up and down staircases, caught glimpses of people in all kinds of uniforms – lawyers, teachers, administrators of crown estates, all of them wearing insignia. They glimpsed ladies, fur coats on hangers; a cold draught brought the smell of cigarette ends. Gurov's heart was throbbing. 'God in heaven!' he thought. 'Why these people, this orchestra?'

And at that moment he suddenly remembered saying to himself, after he had seen Anna Sergeyevna off at the station that evening, that it was all over and that they would never see one another again. But how far they still were from the end!

On the narrow, gloomy staircase with the sign 'Entrance to Circle' she stopped.

'What a fright you gave me!' she exclaimed, breathing heavily, still pale and stunned. 'Oh, what a fright you gave me. I'm barely alive! Why have you come? Why?'

'Please understand, Anna, please understand,' he said hurriedly in an undertone. 'I beg you, *please* understand!'

She looked at him in fear, in supplication – and with love, staring at his face to fix his features more firmly in her mind.

'It's such hell for me!' she went on without listening to him. 'The whole time I've thought only of you. I've existed only by thinking about you. And I wanted to forget, forget. But why have you come?'

On a small landing above them two schoolboys were smoking and looking down, but Gurov didn't care. He drew Anna Sergeyevna to him and started kissing her face, her cheeks, her arms.

'What are you doing? What are you doing?' she cried out in horror, pushing him away. 'We've both gone out of our minds! You *must* leave tonight . . . you must go now . . . I implore you, by all that's holy, I *beg* you . . . Someone's coming . . . !'

Someone was coming up the staircase.

'You *must* go,' Anna Sergeyevna continued, whispering. 'Do you hear, Dmitry Dmitrich? I'll come and see you in Moscow. I've never been happy, I'm unhappy now and I shall never, never be happy! Never! Don't make me suffer even more! I swear I'll come to Moscow. But now we must say goodbye . . . My dear, kind darling, we must part!'

She pressed his hand and swiftly went downstairs, constantly looking back at him – and he could see from her eyes that she really was unhappy. Gurov stayed a while longer, listening hard. And then, when all was quiet, he found his peg and left the theatre.

IV

And Anna Sergeyevna began to visit him in Moscow. Two or three times a month she left S——, telling her husband that she was going to consult a professor about some women's complaint – and her husband neither believed nor disbelieved her. In Moscow she stayed at the Slav Fair Hotel, and the moment she arrived she would send a messenger with a red cap over to Gurov. He would go to her hotel and no one in Moscow knew a thing.

One winter's morning he went to see her as usual (the messenger had called the previous evening but he had been out). With him walked his daughter, whom he wanted to take to school, as it was on the way. A thick wet snow was falling.

'It's three degrees above zero, yet it's snowing,' Gurov told his daughter. 'But it's only warm on the surface of the earth, the temperature's quite different in the upper layers of the atmosphere.'

'Papa, why isn't there thunder in winter?'

And he explained this too, conscious as he spoke that here he was on his way to an assignation, that not a soul knew about it and that probably no one would ever know. He was leading a double life: one was undisguised, plain for all to see and known to everyone who needed to know, full of conventional truths and conventional deception, identical to the lives of his friends and acquaintances; and another which went on in secret. And by some strange, possibly fortuitous chain of circumstances, everything that was important, interesting and necessary for him, where he behaved sincerely and did not deceive himself and which was the very essence of his life – that was conducted in complete secrecy; whereas all that was false about him, the front behind which he hid in order to conceal the truth – for instance, his work at the bank, those quarrels at the club, his notions of an 'inferior breed', his attending anniversary celebrations with his wife – that was plain for all to see. And he judged others by himself, disbelieving what he saw, invariably assuming that everyone's true, most interesting life was carried on under the cloak of secrecy, under the cover of night, as it were. The private, personal life of everyone is grounded in secrecy and this perhaps partly explains why civilized man fusses so neurotically over having this personal secrecy respected.

After taking his daughter to school, Gurov went to the Slav Fair Hotel. He took off his fur coat downstairs, went up and gently tapped at the door. Anna Sergeyevna, wearing his favourite grey dress, exhausted by the journey and by the wait, had been expecting him since the previous evening. She was pale and looked at him unsmiling; but the moment he entered the room she flung herself on his chest. Their kiss was long and lingering, as though they had not seen one another for two years.

'Well, how are things?' he asked. 'What's the news?'

'Wait, I'll tell you in a moment. But not now . . .'

She was unable to speak for crying. Turning away from him she pressed her handkerchief to her eyes.

'Well, let her have a good cry . . . I'll sit down in the meantime', he thought as he sat in the armchair.

Then he rang and ordered some tea. After he had drunk it she was still standing there, facing the window. She wept from the mournful realization that their lives had turned out so sadly. They were meeting in secret, hiding from others, like thieves! Surely their lives were ruined?

'Please stop crying!' he said.

Now he could see quite clearly that this was no short-lived affair – and it was impossible to say when it would finish. Anna Sergeyevna had become even more attached to him, she adored him and it would have been unthinkable of him to tell her that some time all this had to come to an end. And she would not have believed him even if he had.

He went over to her and put his hands on her shoulders, intending to caress her, to joke a little – and then he caught sight of himself in the mirror.

He was already going grey. And he thought it strange that he had aged so much over the past years, had lost his good looks. The shoulders on which his hands were resting were warm and trembling. He felt pity for this life, still so warm and beautiful, but probably about to fade and wither like his own. Why did she love him so? Women had never taken him for what he really was – they didn't love the man himself, but someone who was a figment of their imagination, someone they had been eagerly seeking all their lives. And then, when they realized their mistake, they still loved him. Not one of them had been happy with him. Time passed, he met new women, had affairs, parted, but never once had he been in love. There had been everything else, but there had been no love.

And only now, when his hair had turned grey, had he genuinely, truly fallen in love – for the first time in his life.

Anna Sergeyevna and he loved one another as close intimates, as man and wife, as very dear friends. They thought that fate itself had intended them for each other and it was a mystery why he should have a wife and she a husband. And in fact they were like two birds of passage, male and female, caught and forced to live in separate cages. They forgave one another all they had been ashamed of in the past, forgave everything in the present, and they felt that this love of theirs had transformed them both.

Before, in moments of sadness, he had reassured himself with any kind of argument that happened to enter his head, but now he was not in the mood for arguments: he felt profound pity and wanted to be sincere, tender . . .

'Please stop crying, my sweet,' he said. 'You've had a good cry . . . it's enough . . . Let's talk now – we'll think of something.'

Then they conferred for a long time and wondered how they could free themselves from the need to hide, to deceive, to live in different towns, to see each other only after long intervals. How could they break free from these intolerable chains?

'How? How?' he asked, clutching his head. '*How?*'

And it seemed – given a little more time – a solution would be found and then a new and beautiful life would begin. And both of them clearly realized that the end was far, far away and that the most complicated and difficult part was only just beginning.

THE STORY OF PENGUIN CLASSICS

Before 1946 ... 'Classics' are mainly the domain of academics and students, without readable editions for everyone else. This all changes when a little-known classicist, E. V. Rieu, presents Penguin founder Allen Lane with the translation of Homer's Odyssey that he has been working on and reading to his wife Nelly in his spare time.

1946 The Odyssey becomes the first Penguin Classic published, and promptly sells three million copies. Suddenly, classic books are no longer for the privileged few.

1950s Rieu, now series editor, turns to professional writers for the best modern, readable translations, including Dorothy L. Sayers's *Inferno* and Robert Graves's *The Twelve Caesars*, which revives the salacious original.

1960s 1961 sees the arrival of the Penguin Modern Classics, showcasing the best twentieth-century writers from around the world. Rieu retires in 1964, hailing the Penguin Classics list as 'the greatest educative force of the 20th century'.

1970s A new generation of translators arrives to swell the Penguin Classics ranks, and the list grows to encompass more philosophy, religion, science, history and politics.

1980s The Penguin American Library joins the Classics stable, with titles such as *The Last of the Mohicans* safeguarded. Penguin Classics now offers the most comprehensive library of world literature available.

1990s Penguin Popular Classics are launched, offering readers budget editions of the greatest works of literature. Penguin Audiobooks brings the classics to a listening audience for the first time, and in 1999 the launch of the Penguin Classics website takes them online to an ever larger global readership.

The 21st Century Penguin Classics are rejacketed for the first time in nearly twenty years. This world famous series now consists of more than 1,300 titles, making the widest range of the best books ever written available to millions – and constantly redefining the meaning of what makes a 'classic'.

The Odyssey continues ...

The best books ever written

PENGUIN 🐧 CLASSICS

SINCE 1946